Before

<u>Monster</u>

A little eight year old girl laid in her bed clutching onto her teddy bear in the hope it could keep her safe from the monsters that visited during the dark hours. She knew it couldn't. It couldn't even keep them from her room although she wished it would.

It wasn't every night it happened but it occurred more than it should have done and she didn't understand why.

The door would slowly open and he'd stand there, in the doorway, looking at her lying in her bed across the room. She'd pretend to sleep in the hope he'd leave but he never did. He'd walk in and push the door to before walking over to her bed. He'd sit on the edge of it and move the teddy bear from the little girl's tight grasp before setting it to the side on the floor. She'd open her eyes - this little child - and look at him with a look of fear that he didn't seem to register. If he did - he didn't care.

"Don't need this in our way, do we?" he'd tell her.

She'd pull the blankets up under her chin but she knew it wouldn't stop him from pulling them away if he chose to - and most nights he'd do just that. She'd want to scream. She'd want to cry but he told her that if she said anything, or did anything, he didn't like then he'd tell her mummy and she'd kick her from the house because she was dirty.

"You don't need all these blankets tonight," he'd say. "It's so warm."

He'd pull them off her and look at her pyjamas; a cartoon mouse in a dress on the front of them. He'd look at her and smile.

"I like your pyjamas." he'd say.

The little girl wouldn't reply to him. She'd just lay there, scared. He'd reach out with one hand and gently stroke her face. He'd tell her that, if she did what he asked, she wouldn't have anything to fear from him and that they would have some fun together. She always did what he said. The same hand that stroked her face would work its way down her covered body to her pyjama bottoms. There it would linger a moment before sliding its way between skin and cloth as his other hand did the same with the bottoms he was wearing. As the man's hand moved further down, the little girl couldn't help but flinch at the unwanted touch. She'd never scream - not out loud. Not on nights that went like this… Only on the other nights would she cry out.

The nights didn't follow a similar pattern each time. Sometimes they seemed more tender as if her feelings were being taken into consideration. Other times - when the house was otherwise empty - the actions were more forceful as feelings were damned and sexual needs fulfilled with no fear of being disturbed by anyone.

When mornings came around - and they always did - the little girl would complain to her mother that she didn't feel well but her mother would rarely listen. She'd get her dressed and pack her off to school so she could go to work herself. As the little girl wailed about her health, the monster would just sit there at the breakfast table without a care in the world. His eyes not on his nighttime toy but rather the broadsheet paper laid out before him.

"Is it just me or is the world filled only with doom and gloom these days?" he'd take a sip of his morning coffee. "I swear the whole world is going to hell."

PART ONE

22 Years Later

Standing in front of the mirror in my bathroom applying lipstick for the fourth time today. It has been a busy one for sure, not that I am complaining after yesterday. Yesterday had been deathly quiet with my phone ringing only a couple of times compared to the usual dozen, or so, phone calls I receive in my working hours.

There are many names for what I do for a living; prostitute, lady of the night, working girl, escort, sex worker and whore. My personal preference being 'prostitute' a word which derives from the Latin word prostituta. The term prostitute hides nothing. I like that. No dressing it up as anything more than what it is - and that's taking money in exchange for sexual services.

There are many people out there - in society - who look down their noses at girls such as me and yet my job is the oldest profession in the world. And did you know that estimates place the annual revenue generated by prostitution to be over one hundred billion dollars. Goes to show that no matter how many people out there who frown upon what we do, there are many more who are willing to seek us out for their own gratification. Although experience has also taught me that even some of those who look down upon us, when they're out in the real world, are also the ones who sneak into our arms and vaginas when their friends and co-workers, or even wives, sleep.

I set the lipstick to one side, next to my make-up bag, and took a second to admire myself in the mirror. I look good, just as I should for my clients. Long blonde hair, a healthy size twelve figure with large breasts accentuated by my choice of uplifting bra underneath my short, shiny black dress. Stockings held up by suspenders which disappear underneath said dress giving a tease as to the classy lingerie hidden beneath the outer layer. I look both classy and slutty; the latter being important as I need to win over the man's primal instinct as soon as I open the door to them. Once they're thinking 'sex' - they're like putty in my hands.

I walked through to the bedroom and checked everything was in its place; condoms on the side, next to the bed. Next to the condoms a bottle of strawberry flavoured lubricant - a handful of which has already been applied to my pussy. Equally as important as getting the client to start thinking about sex as soon as they walk through the door is getting them to think they've made you wet. Those two factors alone are enough to get a man close to the edge. The quicker they're spent, the quicker they leave - if you're looking to do the job with minimal effort and fuss.

Some girls offer a service which affords the man multiple orgasms. As long as they can achieve it they can ejaculate as many times as they want. Experience has taught me, unless they've booked in for a few hours, they're usually happy with the one orgasm and even then, with some of the more nervous of punters, this can be difficult to reach.

Thankfully we don't just have to rely on our hands, mouths and cunts - and, in the case of some girls, assholes. We have the luxury of many toys at our disposal to bring into the bedroom; butt-plugs, vibrators, eggs, whips, blindfolds, gags, clamps, strap-ons, dildos to name but a few that I keep in a plastic box underneath my bed within easy reach with a duplicate collection, although maybe not quite as big, in a large over the shoulder bag for appointments sought on an out-call basis.

In-call appointments are run from home, out-call appointments from the customer's home or hotel.

Over the years I have learned many skills to aid me with my job and help me stand out amongst the ever-growing surge of new girls coming in from overseas with only a basic grasp of the English language but a thirst for money and cock. My list of services provided is detailed on my personal page on one of the many escorting sites on the world wide web and runs as follows: BDSM, CIM (cum in mouth), Deep Throat, Dinner Dates, Disabled Clients, Domination, Face Sitting, Facials, Fetish, FFM 3Somes, Sploshing (food sex), French Kissing (at my discretion), hand relief, humiliation (giving), lapdancing, massage, oral, period play, pole dancing, prostate massage, receiving oral, rimming, role play and fantasy, smoking (fetish), spanking (giving), strap on, striptease, sub games, swallow, tie and tease, toys, travel companion, uniforms, water sports (giving). Sometimes I have no choice but to offer them whatever they want but wherever possible I like to offer a different kind of service to the other girls out there working their way in the industry. This service isn't aimed at the men who come to see me. It's aimed at the women who tolerate them out there in the real-world. It's a service I offer the wives and girlfriends, long-term partners. It's a service for the women who aren't aware their partners are cheating on them with a string of sexual encounters with ladies of the night. It's a service offered to eliminate the hurt they feel when they find out about the secret life their partner is leading...

It's a service whereby I end the lives of the miserable fucks who come to see me.

I have two bags that I can take to my appointments.

The first bag is for the appointments that I have to go through with - usually the ones in the hotels which are done with eyes closed and cunt well-lubed. I like to think of them as my 'keeping up appearances' sessions. The ones which lead the men to go home and - on the promise of a discount the next time they see me - write a field report (like a feedback form) for other men to see and read. Field reports are good. They help prove to men that they can trust that I am good at my job and safe to book. So many bad girls out there with bad feedback, offering sub-par sessions at still high prices. If I do see a punter and the appointment leads to them leaving with a smile on their face as opposed to a gash across their throat, I offer them money off if they come back and see me again. The discount offered to the punters who I don't kill on their appointment; a lure to bring them back for a second session. One which they don't tend to walk away from.

The second bag is for the appointments that do not end in the client's happy ending. It's for the appointments which end in nothing but their pain, misery and - ultimately - death. The sessions which give their partners some much deserved freedom. Freedom with which they can go out and find a real man who actually gives a damn about them.

No prizes for guessing which is my favourite kind of appointment.

Right on cue there was a heavy knock on the front door of my otherwise quiet home. An in-call appointment. My personal favourite as it means there are no maids to interrupt us (as has happened in a hotel before now) and no nosy neighbours who might raise the alarm upon hearing the screams - be they screams of pleasure or screams of terror. No need to gag the appointment. Get to let this one scream.

I quickly put some high heels on as the appointment knocked on the door again. He can wait a moment, he knows I am in, having already answered his text message with the exact location of my house. I always get them to park a few roads away before giving them the address. Saves them knocking on the door any earlier when I'm trying to get ready. It's funny how a man can often run late for things he has no interest in but the moment he is onto a promise - he shows up early with nothing more than an erection and a smile.

With the high heels on, accentuating my long legs, I walked down the stairs and to the front door. I opened it up and revealed a dark haired man who looked to be in his late twenties - around the age I liked to tell the clients I was at. He could have been a little younger. As he smiled and said hello, stepping into the house, all I could think was that he wouldn't be getting any older.

I closed the door.

"Can I get you a drink?" I asked my client as I walked him through to the living room.

He had called himself Jon in the original email booking he sent me. Whether that was his real name or not I'll never know. Truth be told, I don't care anyway. It's not as though I give them my true identity so why should they give me theirs?

"I'm okay, thank you."

There are two types of client. The clients who bring their own bottle of drink - always alcoholic despite having driven to the appointment - and the ones who bring nothing and refuse everything; no doubt worried the drinking time will be coming out of their allotted booking time.

In the living room he took a seat. He looked nervous. I remembered the message he had sent me on his initial approach. He had wanted to do this for a while - by 'this' I guessed he meant having sex with a working girl as opposed to him calling me 'this' - but he hadn't had the bottle to do so. He had told me he felt awkward, embarrassed almost. It's funny. In this line of work you hear that a lot, even from people you wouldn't expect to hear it from; the ones who show up in the fancy Aston Martins and expensive suits - people who appear to be in a position of power out there in the real world.

"Oh," the man suddenly remembered the money. He fished in his pocket and pulled out a wad of notes.

"In your message you said you weren't sure whether you wanted an hour or two," I reminded him. Need to make it clear now. Don't want to get towards the end of the hour only for him to point out he had wanted two. I know what you're thinking: Why does it matter if I'm going to kill him? It doesn't matter. I can kill him in as little or long a time as I want but it is important to stay in practice for how a real appointment goes. The last thing I want to do is get stuck with a client I have to service properly and fall into a trap of being there for longer than they had paid or something equally as frustrating. It's always best to stay on the ball, so to speak. I didn't need him to answer. I could feel from the money that it was one hour.

"If it's okay can we see how things go today with one hour and then - maybe - I could see you again another day?"

"Sure," I lied.

I set the money to one side and sat down next to him and crossed my legs with them pointed in his direction. My hand rested on his leg as I broke out the small chat. He squirmed at my touch. This is the 'putting the client at ease' part of the appointment. If they're not at ease then it will be harder for them to get an erection when the time comes which, in turn, means I have to put in more of an effort. I literally have a couple of minutes to make these people feel at home. More than that - I have a couple of minutes to make them feel as though they're with a partner. At the very least someone who likes them.

"Sorry, I'm a little nervous," he said. "Never done this before."

"Relax. It's fine. I promise I don't bite."

No biting; an easy promise to keep but the same can't be said for 'maiming'.

"So what kind of thing do you like? Your message didn't give me much to go on," I purred. Again he shifted in his seat in clear discomfort. I couldn't help but laugh, "You really have done nothing like this before, have you?"

He shook his head and smiled nervously, "No. Never. First time."

"Just relax. It'll be fine. And once you get into the swing of things, you won't remember why you were so nervous to begin with. Trust me. Just tell me what you like and I'll take it from there," I offered.

"Do you mind if we just talk a little while?" he asked.

I was a little taken aback by his request. Usually the men I seemed to attract from the website were keen to skip conversation completely and just get down to business. Some even tried putting their stinking tongues down my throat before I had even the chance to put the money to one side. I'd be standing there with the notes in my hands, a surprised look on my face and they'd be standing there with an erection between their legs, their tongue forcing its way into my closed mouth and a hand on my arse. And people say romance is dead.

"What would you like to talk about?" I asked.

All thoughts of servicing the man dissipated from my mind as I realised there was a good chance I was about to become more of a counsellor than a sex therapist.

"You," he said.

Again, his answer took me by surprise.

"Well, okay."

Luckily I had a back-story to the character I pretended to be when clients asked me questions I deemed as being too personal to answer with the truth. It's hard remembering all the little facts when you first start in the business but once you get into it and you've been doing it for a few years - it soon becomes second nature. If anything it gets trickier remembering what the truth is. Well, I say that, but I'll never forget what started me off on this path. It's impossible to put that from my mind. God knows I have tried.

His first question, "Of all the things you could be in life, why'd you choose to do this job?"

He wasn't the first person to ask the question and I'm sure he won't be the last. I find it amusing that these men pay for the services I offer them behind closed doors, away from their girlfriends and wives, and yet they're always puzzled as to why I do it. It's almost as though they're saying it is perfectly acceptable for them to pay for sex but it's wrong for someone to want to take money for it.

I sighed as the lie started formulating in my mind.

Not all girls in this industry are damaged. I'm sure there are some who genuinely do it for the love of the sex and the addiction to the money available; the story I was about to give my client was that I had started doing it to pay my way through university and that one thing had lead to another and here I was - five years later, with a degree, still offering the services to the men who sought them. He looked suitably impressed by my lie - at least the part about the degree anyway. Men are more likely to want to sleep with women who appear intelligent as opposed to those who were continually raped by their own father from the age of eight years old.

"A degree? What in? That's great."

"English Literature," was the first thing that popped into my mind. Not sure why, I hated English when I was at school.

"Impressive. I didn't get past college," he said.

He should count himself lucky. I didn't even get the opportunity of going to college.

"You must be really brave though," he said out of the blue.

"What do you mean? Why would you say that?" I asked him.

"It's easy for men who book you. They can see pictures of you on the Internet before they make an appointment. Sure the faces might be blurred out but the shape of the girl is enough to see and enough to help them determine whether they'd find the lady sexy. Choosing to be a working girl - you don't get a choice in who you see. It's just a question of pot-luck when you open the door. That's brave. I couldn't do it. Hard to imagine. Especially the first time..."

⋏

I opened the front door. My heart was racing as much as it had been when I replied to the man's booking request; one hour, girlfriend experience. The man had his back to me. He turned around. Older gentleman. Maybe twenty years my senior if I am being generous. Nicely dressed but could already tell he was wearing far too much aftershave. Better than stinking of sweat, I guess. He saw me and smiled. Yellow teeth, nicotine stained. Can't have it all I suppose. Grateful that my service page lists French Kissing at my discretion.

"Hi," I backed up from the doorway and he stepped in, nearly gassing me in the sweet scent of his aftershave. "You found the house with no problems then?" I asked.

"Certainly did."

I closed the door.

"Can I get you a drink?"

"No. Thank you."

I turned around and jumped when I realised he was standing close to me. He smiled again as he pulled me close to him with his hands around my buttocks.

"You look sexy," he smiled.

"Thank you." I put my hands on his chest and smiled sweetly at him, "Want to get the paperwork out of the way and come upstairs?"

My first appointment. I thought it was going to be awkward asking for the cash but it wasn't. As soon as I felt the stranger's hands on my body I remembered why I was doing this in the first place. Money. His over-eagerness probably helped me, as did the lack of wanting a drink. Had he wanted some kind of liquid refreshments and started with a 'normal' conversation, I may have struggled a little more.

✦

"Were you even nervous?" Jon asked me. An unusual infatuation with my working life temporarily made me think he was a journalist looking for a story. It's only when I remembered this kind of story had been covered thousands of times before that I realised was being stupid. "The first time you saw someone," he reiterated.

I laughed and tried to turn his curiosity away from the questions he was asking, "Did you want to be a male escort?"

He looked shocked, "What? No." He paused a second, "Why?"

"Lot of questions. Sounded like you wanted to move into the industry." I could see from his face that this wasn't the case. Maybe he wanted to know more about how I ticked before taking the final plunge of actually sleeping with me? Whatever his motives - turning the tables back on him seemed to make him more uncomfortable. Bad move. "I was just teasing you," I said.

"Oh. Right. Good one." He smiled. "So what was it like?" he asked.

"What was what like?"

"The first time."

"Why do you want to know?"

"Just curious."

▲

We moved into the bedroom. The client turned to me as soon as I had closed the bedroom door. A look on his face suggested he was keen to touch me and get things started. I was dressed in the finest of lingerie - the best bra and underwear set that I owned - but I could see that, in his eyes, I was already undressed. He licked his lips. I did my best not to shudder.

"Can't very well get far with all those clothes on," I told him.

The sooner we start, the sooner we finish. Just get it done. Remember why I am doing it. Bills to pay. Cupboards are empty. Credit card debt mounting up. Fired from yet another nine to five job. I watched from the door as the man started to undress. He started with his white shirt, undoing all of the buttons. He took it off and threw it to the corner of the room before starting to undo his belt. In my mind I imagined him to be someone else. A film star. Every time I thought I'd settled on picturing one star, another popped into my head and so it came to be he was flitting from face to face and body to body in my mind's eye.

His trousers were kicked over to where his shirt landed, as were his underpants. He was standing there, wrinkles and all, stroking his semi-erect penis as he looked at my body.

"Where do you want me?" he asked.

Before he had even arrived and presented himself at my front door, I knew I would never be able to forget him. There was no way I could forget my first client. The smile on his face now - a filthy yellow stained sleazy grin - just reiterated the impossibility of forgetting and pulled my mind back to reality with a bump. Gone are the film stars. Here to stay is the dirty old man. I glanced down to his erection. My eyes drawn by a shine coming from a wedding band on his finger. I tried to put it from my mind.

"Lay on your front?"

The man did as he was asked and laid on his front, his head on my pillow. Seeing his head pressed against my clean pillow was the first time I had even thought about the bedding. This was my bed. I slept in it. And yet here was a stranger lying upon it and here we were - about to do a whole lot more. I imagined the sweat dripping from his wrinkled body, soaking the sheets. I imagined his pre-cum now pooling there as he waited for my touch. I can't believe I didn't think about it sooner. Too late to worry about it now. From this moment on - this bedding is my work bedding. I'll buy a fresh set for me tomorrow with the profits from the night - not that there are many profits from this evening's appointment if I am being sensible. Bills to pay, debts to clear. Stuff them. I need clean bedding. I tried to force the thoughts from my mind as I crossed the room and climbed onto the bed, straddling his legs in the process. He sighed as I leaned forward and started to rub his back.

"I'm not too heavy, am I?" I asked.

"No. Not at all. It's nice."

Film star. Johnny Depp. Robert Downey Jnr. Brad Pitt. The man squirmed underneath me and managed to twist himself around so that he was on his back. My touch had clearly had the desired effect. I started rubbing his chest.

"Someone is pleased to see me," I smiled. I was conscious of the smile. I had been practicing it all night as I stood in front of the bathroom mirror for possibly longer than strictly necessary but I had to make sure people believed it. If they didn't - they wouldn't come back and the bills would continue to grow.

I felt the man buck his body underneath me. A slight arching of his back forcing his penis towards me. I knew what he wanted. I knew what part of his body he wanted to feel my touch upon. I stroked down his chest and gently brushed my fingers over his penis. He sighed again as his cock twitched to my touch. I looked up to his face. His eyes were closed. I kept focused on his expression as I nervously gripped his hard-on with my right hand. My left had gently working his testicles in a soft squeezing motion. He continued to sigh. A smile on his face. Eyes still shut. It was important to concentrate on his expression. I figured some men might be uncomfortable voicing their concerns if you do something wrong but it's rare that - when someone is completely relaxed – that their expression would hide a sudden moment of discomfort. There was no such discomfort here. I started to stroke up and down harder now, building to a steady rhythm. The man's sighs matched the strokes. A few minutes passed by and I was starting to get arm ache but couldn't stop. I read in a book that if you stop - the man's building orgasm is potentially put back to square one. I just want this over with.

"Put it in your mouth," he pleaded.

I glanced down to his cut cock. It looked clean enough but I still wasn't keen. I looked back up to his face. He was staring right at me, an expectant look on his face. I leaned over to the bedside cabinet and reached for a condom. I tore the wrapper off, using my teeth, and rolled it down his penis. I waited for him to voice a complaint; my page said I offer Oral Without Protection at my discretion. To my surprise, he didn't say anything. Just closed his eyes again as I started sucking. His hands - either side of his body, stretched out - grasped the duvet tightly and didn't let go. When my head was at the top of his cock's head, I took a hold of it in my right hand and started wanking it as I flicked my tongue back and forth on his helmet. He groaned in pleasure.

"Sit on my face!" he pleaded.

I stopped what I was doing long enough to slide my knickers off. He made a funny noise from his throat as he viewed my naked pussy for the first time. Without further words, I climbed on top of him and lowered myself over his face as per his request. He strained his head upwards, by cranking his neck, and - less than a second later - I felt his tongue against my lips. I put him in my mouth again as I continued the motion of mouth and hand around his penis. As I continued to suck and wank, I tried my best to ignore his tongue inside of me.

All I could picture were his yellow teeth. All I could think about was what kind of state was his tongue in? I gagged - a combination of a sudden thrust from him forcing his cock's head to the back of my throat and the thought of his stinking tongue spreading it's saliva up inside of me.

A

"Wouldn't you rather experience your own first time?" I asked.

Jon shifted in his seat as I ran my hand up his leg and onto his crotch. A gentle squeeze and I could feel that he wasn't quite ready yet. Too soft.

"You can touch me if you want," I purred.

I took his hand and moved it onto my breast. A little encouragement from my own hand, and he was soon gently squeezing my breast. My other hand felt him start to stiffen where it really counted. He coughed and pulled his hand away. I didn't move mine as I continued to grope him in the hope of getting him hard. I knew that - as soon as the blood was rushing to his erection - he'd not be as keen to ask questions about the job and more intent with going with the flow.

"Is that alright?" I asked.

He closed his eyes for a moment and put his head back on the settee - enjoying the sensation of my hand rubbing him through his jeans. He was hard now. I slid off the settee and onto the floor in front of him on my knees. I stopped groping him for a second and started working on his jean's buttons. A professional; it didn't take long and he was soon exposed. I moved in closer and gently breathed warm air onto his cock. It twitched in anticipation. With no warning he sat bolt upright and pushed me away forcibly. I fell back onto my bum, a bemused look on my face.

"I'm sorry," he said, "I'm not ready..."

He started to adjust himself; putting his penis back into his pants and doing them up again as I sat up.

"Really? Because - from where I was - you looked ready."

"It's not that. I'm sorry. I think I've made a mistake."

He stood up and finished tucking himself in. I too stood up.

"A mistake?"

"I shouldn't have come here. I'm sorry."

He walked out of the lounge door and down the hallway. I stood for a moment - confused as to what was happening - and gave chase.

"Wait a minute. You've paid for an hour. If you're not ready for sex, we can just talk. If that's what you want that's fine."

"I'm sorry. I can't."

He opened the front door and stepped onto my drive.

"At least take your money back," I called after him. He didn't turn back for it though. He got into his beat up old car and reversed out of the drive and onto the road. A quick gear change and he wheel-spun away.

I don't recall how many men I have seen in this line of work. It's hard to keep track of them. I'm not sure how many I have slept with compared to how many I have disposed of and yet this was the first time - ever - that an appointment had ended in such a way. A strange feeling washed over me. I actually felt bad for him. A lad so shy he couldn't stand the thought of me touching him.

I closed the front door, wondering what I had done that was so wrong to drive him away. I walked from the hallway into the living room where Jon had previously stormed from his comfortable position on the sofa. I looked out of the window curious to see whether he had turned around at the end of the road and come back - if only for the money he had left behind. Not a soul out there.

I walked back over to the settee and crashed onto it. I do not necessarily enjoy the job that I found myself doing other than when the appointments end by setting free the clients' partners but - even so - having someone run out of your appointment wasn't good for a girl's self-confidence. Usually - the normal appointments - boost a girl's confidence more than you could imagine. Here are these men that want to sleep with you. Not only that - they're happy to pay for the privilege of doing so. And usually - the whole time - they're telling you how fucking amazing you are. They leave with a smile on their faces and you close the door on them, a smile on yours. Not because of the sexual satisfaction you've received - those appointments are few and far between - but because you feel appreciated as a woman.

I felt the old man's hands on my buttocks as I continued to push my sopping pussy down onto his face whilst working his shaft with both hand and mouth. He pushed my bum up so that I was no longer suffocating him.

"I'm coming," he moaned.

I increased both pressure and rhythm until I felt his penis throb in my mouth. He sighed with pleasure as it continued to throb - thick ejaculate filling the teat of the condom enveloping his manhood.

"S-s-stop," he sighed. A little laugh. "Sensitive."

I rolled off him and laid next to his body; his face next to my lower half and my face next to his.

"That was amazing," he laughed. "I needed that. Thank you."

He smiled. Those yellow teeth. I smiled back, remembering the amount of practice I had put in the night before perfecting it for moments like this. I climbed from the bed and reached for a packet of wet wipes which were situated next to the condom packet. I pulled one out and used it on my undercarriage. I handed the rest to him. I'll never forget his smile - his rank teeth - but I can't even remember his name. He pulled the condom off and threw it to the side as though it were just a piece of rubbish. Fair enough it was - but as I watched it dribble onto the mattress - I couldn't help but wish he had wrapped it up in one of the wet wipes first. Just as I had wiped myself down, he did the same to himself. When he was done, I took the wipes from him and threw them into a small bin by the bed. He thanked me.

"You're going to cost me a lot of money, I can tell."

He laughed.

I smiled at him as though his words were a pleasure to hear but - inside - I was dying. The thought of his tongue inside of me made me feel sick. The thought of him doing anything else to me - doesn't bear thinking about.

He laughed again, "Hopefully the wife won't notice the money going from the joint account."

I didn't say anything. The man sat up and reached for his underpants. He slid them on.

"You're married?" I asked him.

He nodded, "On paper. Cost me more to leave than just put up with her."

I wanted to snap at him for the way he was talking about his wife but it wasn't my place to do so.

"What does she do?" I asked.

"Bleeds me dry," he laughed. "She doesn't do anything. Stays at home whilst I go out and bring the money in. Used to have a job but - yeah - gave that up."

The man pulled his trousers on and reached for his shirt. I felt sorry for his wife. I couldn't help but wonder if she knew of her husband's extra-curricular activities or whether she was blind to it all. Can't ask him. Too personal. He was dressed now.

"Oh to be younger again." He was staring at my body. "Once is more than enough for one day though."

"Too bad," I lied. I'm glad he was done. I couldn't wait for him to get out of the house so I could burn the bedsheets. Possibly even the room.

"There's always next time," he smiled. Yellow teeth. "Right... Well... Thank you then."

I climbed off the bed and he leaned in for a kiss. Thankfully he planted it on my cheek. I kissed his. Can always wash as soon as he leaves.

"You're very welcome. And thank you for coming to see me," I told him.

"It was my pleasure."

And it was his. All his.

I walked him down the stairs and to the front door which I wasted no time in opening. I felt a weight lift off my shoulders as he stepped out - onto the driveway.

He turned back to me, "Thanks again."

"You're welcome."

"Listen, I noticed you didn't have any reviews on your page. Did you not want them?"

"I'm new to the game. No one has left any yet."

"They really do help people like me make our minds up. If it weren't for your alluring pictures, I wouldn't have given you a punt..."

I didn't know what to say in response to that.

"... Would you like for me to leave a review for you?" he asked.

"Yes! That would be great! Thank you!"

My debt level and job prospects dictated a need to do the job more than the one time - whether I wanted to or not - and I was well aware of the necessity to have reports written about me by the men who came to see me. Going by the fact my phone had been ringing non-stop since the page went live, and the emails were flooding through, I'm not sure how important the reports were but - regardless - it couldn't hurt.

"Consider it done!" he smiled again.

Yellow teeth.

That's what I'll call him: Yellow Teeth.

Pleasant enough, strong aftershave - bad oral hygiene. Notes for my diary on the off-chance he books me again. Easy to remember him with a nick-name. Especially as I can't remember his real name and it's only been 24 hours since he initially booked me.

"Maybe you can give me a little discount as a thank you, next time I see you?" he suggested.

I didn't know what to say to him. I didn't want to do the job for less money. Looking around the other pages on the website - the prices I charged were average for the area. I didn't want to lower them.

"Maybe," I said after a pause.

"I'll see you soon."

He blew me a kiss - an act which made my body turn cold - as he turned to his nice car. I stood there, in the doorway, as I watched him climb in and start the motor up. He tooted his horn as he pulled from the drive and headed off down the road. I closed the front door and turned my back on it. A huge sigh of relief. I hadn't been certain I was going to be able to go through with it but I had. I wasn't sure whether I should feel proud of that fact or not. I hurried through to the living room where I had earlier stashed the money - after making him wait for 'two seconds' in the hallway as I did so. I snatched it from the bookcase where I had hidden it and flicked through it. The smell of the money. It had been so long since I had this much in my hands. One hundred and fifty pounds in a mixture and tens and twenties. Mostly tens. Not a lot of money to some people but to me - it might as well have been a thousand pounds. I couldn't help but laugh as I flicked through the notes again before tossing them up into the air. They danced through the air as they fell slowly spiraling to the floor. In my head I had already spent the cash on new clothes and food. In reality it would go towards the mounting bills.

A job well done.

$$\blacktriangle$$

I put Jon's money into the pot hidden in the kitchen. A wad of notes already saved in there. My debt had been cleared a long time ago; a few years at least and now the money was just going into my own savings scheme. Temptation was to blow the lot but I knew one day there was a chance I'd have to grab a bag and disappear. Can't very well do that if you've spent everything you have accumulated over the years. As I closed the lid on the pot, I still felt guilty about taking his money. Can't help but wonder what would have happened had he stayed and wasted his whole appointment talking about the job. I didn't even know if he had a girlfriend, or wife, in the outside world - something which is a pre-requisite that I look for before I end them. They have a partner, they die. Simple as that. Their partner gets to move on thinking their other half has simply vanished on them. The men who don't have a partner - the ones who see me because it is convenient to them or because they haven't been lucky enough to find love in the real world - they're the ones I tend to go easy on. Sometimes. I guess it all depends on my mood and how they treat me at the end of the day. But - they could be the kindest person in the world - they have a partner, they're dead.

I set the pot back onto the shelf amongst the various pots and pans I had purchased over the years and wandered into my office space. A small room opposite the living room. Just about big enough for a small swivel chair and computer workstation; screen on the table-top and base unit tucked to the side on the floor whirring away. A quick push of the mouse and the screen fired up - already loaded onto my personal page on the bigger escorting site. A quick refresh on the screen and five messages pinged up in my inbox.

No rest for the wicked.

My heart skipped a beat when I read the sender of the top message. It was Jon. Less than five minutes ago. He must have literally parked up at the end of the street and sent it from his mobile phone. I opened it, unsure of what to

expect, and read the contents. An apology. He stated that he wanted to see me, and that he wanted an appointment, but was overcome with shyness. He asked if I minded seeing him again for a second session - one which, in his words, would hopefully reach the conclusion he initially intended. He didn't state what that conclusion was nor did I really need him to. I knew what he meant. He wanted the big 'O', like so many men before him. My heart told me to ignore the message, maybe even delete it. The guy clearly wasn't ready for this industry. Too shy. Too many emotions. This game can take people like that and mess with their heads badly. They come for their appointments, they have the intercourse they're looking for and then they leave but the encounter isn't over for them. These are the kind of people who go away and continue thinking about the girl they had just laid with. Their heads start playing mind games with them. No longer was the appointment nothing more than a business transaction, now it was something deeper. The girl loved the boy. And he loved her. This kind of situation is referred to as the Pretty Woman Syndrome. The client starts thinking he can save the girl from the life she is leading and that they'll move in together and live happily ever after in their own private worlds. It's happened before and I'm sure it will happen again. And going from some of the other girls' reports; I know I am not the only one to experience this. So, yes, my heart told me to ignore the message. My brain - on the other hand - pointed out that it was easy money. Rude not to.

BEFORE

<u>Monster</u>

The little girl was not so little anymore. Four years had passed by. Twelve years old now and still terrified of speaking up against the night-time monster who'd creep into her room stinking of alcohol and filled with lust. Same touch as before; tender and gentle when the mother was bathing in the other room and hard and fast when she was out working late - like tonight.

The little girl would lie awake at night waiting for the monster to come crawling up to her bed from the doorway; same stink, same look. Tonight was to be no different and it wasn't long after saying goodnight that her door slowly creaked open.

"Are you awake?" the monster slurred from the bedroom door, bottle still in hand.

She didn't answer. She never did. She knew it would make no difference. He was coming in regardless. He always did. The monster stepped in, on cue, and quietly pushed the door shut with his free hand. It took a swig from the bottle and made its way across the room to where she laid. She turned onto her side with her back to him in the hope of being left alone. He never did leave her alone. It just encouraged him to touch her in other places.

"You were looking very pretty tonight," the monster's voice was hushed.

She didn't thank him for the compliment. She closed her eyes as she heard the bottle touch upon the carpet, where he placed it. She held her breath as she waited for what she knew was coming. His touch landed upon her bottom. She bit her bottom lip to stop herself from screaming out.

"Very pretty indeed," the monster continued.

She remained silent, conscious of his touch, his breath and the sound of her own heavy heartbeat.

"Your mother tells me you did well in your exams. That's good. Got into the school you wanted to. She's proud of you. So am I. I even got you a little present."

It was a trick. She knew it was trick. It hadn't been the first time he had used the line on her. She didn't dare to turn around to look at him.

"I have it here in fact," the monster continued.

She wouldn't turn around. She just closed her eyes tighter and wished him dead.

"What you don't want your present?" he asked. "You'll like it, I promise."

Reluctantly she rolled over to see what he had with him. Nothing in his hands. He reached into his pocket and pulled out a small silver foil. A condom.

"It's strawberry," he said. "It's your favourite."

He used both hands to tear the wrapper open. He took out the rubber and put the wrapper back into his pocket so as not to accidentally leave it lying around. He smelt the condom and held it out for her to do the same.

"Smell it."

She nervously leaned forward and sniffed it. She flinched away, disgusted by the smell.

"You don't like the smell?"

She shook her head.

"You don't think it smells like strawberries?"

She shook her head.

The monster stood up and undid his trousers before letting them drop to the floor. His erection stood proud inches from the little girl's body. The monster rolled the condom over his shaft and squeezed the air from the teat at the end.

"Lick it," he said. "See if it tastes more like strawberries than it smells."

The little girl leaned her head forward nervously.

"Here comes the train! Choo Choo!" the monster laughed.

The little girl closed her eyes and wrapped her mouth around the strawberry flavoured rubber. Her eyes remained firmly shut as the monster held her head there for a second before encouraging her to move back and forwards.

"You like your present?" the monster sighed.

PART TWO

18 Years Later

Random Meetings

Jon spent the first five minutes of our second appointment together apologising for the previous day. When he finally believed that I was fine with it and had accepted his apology - he moved straight on to questions about the job. At least this time I had managed to get him upstairs and into the bedroom.

"Aren't you ever scared?" he asked.

We were lying on the bed together. A slight gap between us that wasn't there when I initially laid next to him. He had made that gap. Still too nervous to want to feel my touch. I didn't push it.

"More questions?" I laughed.

"Sorry…"

"No, it's fine."

"Just curious as to what you do."

"Your time."

He hesitated a moment as though waiting for me to answer the question originally posed.

He asked again, "Aren't you ever scared?"

I shook my head.

"No." I paused a moment, "Should I be?"

"Of me?" he laughed. "No."

My answer had been a lie. I had been scared on more than one occasion. The majority of the men who came into the house - or invited me to theirs - were friendly enough. For some of them it was painfully obvious to see why they'd need to pay for the services of a working girl such as myself but some of the men - the way they looked, the way they spoke, the air of confidence they had about themselves; they could have had anyone they wanted. But there were other clients who were just downright creepy. From the way they talked, the way they walked - everything about them made my blood run cold. And it was worse when they smiled.

Something so sinister about them.

Dead eyes.

Inhuman.

Around those men I felt uneasy. I felt uncomfortable and - since the first time I had had an appointment with one of that 'type' – I had felt guarded.

He was just looking at me, smiling. I thought that - maybe - he was hard of hearing and didn't hear me when I asked for the money so I asked again. He slowly shook his head.

"Sorry, love, no cash on me. Haven't been to the bank."

"I'm sorry?"

I shifted on my feet awkwardly - unsure as to whether he was joking around or not. I felt my heartbeat rise a notch.

"Honestly now - do I look like the sort of person who'd pay for it?"

"Then what are you doing here?"

His smile broadened.

"I think you should leave," I said.

I opened the front door and held it there, hoping he'd do as I instructed. He didn't move.

"What's your problem?" I hissed.

"My problem? People like you - that's what my problem is. Girls who think they have the right to charge men for sex. What, you think you're something so special that a man should pay to be with you? Is that it? You're not. You're the lowest of the low. You're a whore. A slut."

I didn't want to point out to him that a slut was someone who'd put out for free. I was a whore - yes. A business woman was a kinder of way of putting it. But he wasn't trying to be kind. He was trying to be cruel and hateful. His mannerisms changed and the smile had long since faded from his gaunt face.

"I think you should leave."

He shook his head.

"I'm going nowhere. Not until I've taught you a lesson."

I noticed the man's left hand clench into a tight ball. I backed away, slowly, wondering whether I could get out of the house before he had a chance to grab me.

"Where do you think you're going?" he said.

Even his voice had changed now.

Meaner.

Monotone.

I went to answer him but was struck hard across the jaw before I had a chance to even open my mouth. I dropped to the floor, my eyes welling up. My jaw was stinging so bad that I couldn't even scream out in agony. I looked up only to see his fist fly towards me. It connected with my mouth. How it didn't knock some teeth out I'll never know. I fell back against the wall, banging my head.

Ringing in my ears.

Stars before my eyes. My eyes that I kept closed to hide from any more blows. Didn't want to see them coming. No blows rained down upon me. I felt his hand grab at my hair. He twisted it so that the strands of hair wrapped around him. A sharp tug and I slid away from the front door and down the hallway. He let me go. I didn't move as I heard his footsteps lead away from me. A second later and the front door slammed. Just him and me.

Just him and me.

I opened my eyes. He was standing before me. Blood on his hands. Blood in my mouth. I spat it out as he pulled himself free from his trousers. Penis standing to attention.

I closed my eyes again.

A monster standing in front of me just as I had seen one stand in a similar position before, back when I was innocent. No duvet to hide behind. No teddy bear to protect me. Just me, him and an unwanted erection.

"We can do this the easy way, or the hard way."

I pulled my knickers to one side, exposing my shaved pussy. He nodded, smiled, and - without so much as a word - kicked me as hard as he could.

⚔

"Never scared? That's good. I'm happy for you. Can't imagine it's the safest job to do, what with inviting strangers into your house…"

I shook thoughts of the violent clients from my mind and answered him as best as I could.

"A lot of the clients that book me have their own feedback too that I can see. Usually it's enough of an indicator as to whether I see them."

"I didn't have any," Jon pointed out.

"Not all of them do," I said, "then it's just a question of gut instinct; how they come across in their messages…"

"So I guess I came across like a nice bloke," he laughed.

"Doesn't this job get in the way of meeting someone for yourself though?" he asked.

Another question.

"New game," I said, "in order to ask a question, you need to remove an item of clothing."

At least if he was in a state of undress, he couldn't just run out of the appointment again. He'd have to put his clothes on - giving me the chance to talk to him and find out why he is trying to leave.

"I'm not sure…"

"Those are the rules."

I was smiling at him, keeping things sweet so as not to scare him. Not sure what I'd do if he left the appointment again only to message me for a third try at a session. Probably have to turn him down. Talking to him now, he clearly has confidence issues. He is shy. Painfully so. Most likely a virgin. Unlike some of my other clients, he can walk away from the appointment with a smile on his face. He deserves a good time. A confidence boost which might hopefully help him out in the real world. He doesn't deserve to be punished. If I can get him in a state of undress; we'll be one step closer to an actual appointment. He leaned forward and took his shirt off. A nice enough physique hidden underneath. Not quite a six pack but definitely some definition there.

"What was the question again?" momentarily distracted.

"Doesn't this job get in the way of meeting someone?"

"I meet lots of people."

Some of whom live to tell the tale. Some of whom don't.

"But you can't form a relationship if you're sleeping with men though. Don't you ever get lonely?"

"Sounds like another question to me."

I looked at his clothes wondering which item he'd remove next.

"Not a question. An observation. Rhetorical question at best," he said.

The truth of the matter was I didn't want to meet anyone. I liked living by myself. I was used to it. No one to disappoint. No one to let down. No lives to ruin. I had a family once and lost them all. I don't want to be in that position again. The job suited me just fine - now that I was used to it. I get to see people, I get to talk to them. I get to have intimacy which is sometimes nice and wanted and I get to feel good about myself when I put an end to a man's cheating ways. It took a while for me to get to this stage of my life but I am happy with where I'm at now.

Relationships just confuse things.

Things get messy.

"So what can I do for you today?" I asked hoping to move the appointment back on track. "Sorry. Broke my own rules. That was a question. Fair is fair…"

I sat up and removed my bra exposing my breasts. The cold air helped my nipples stand to attention giving the false impression of being turned on. He just laid there with his mouth agape, unsure - no doubt - of what to say.

"You can touch them if you want?"

I could see that he wanted to. He was just too nervous to make a move, that's all. I took hold of his hand and guided it towards my breast. A repeat of the day before.

"You've paid your money. You're allowed to touch."

I didn't move my hand from his. I kept it there so he had no choice but to touch my breast. He was staring at it nervously. He looked awkward.

"You like?"

He nodded.

"What about the other one? It's getting lonely."

I took hold of his other hand and placed it onto my other tit. He took a deep breath in and held it.

"It's okay. Relax. This is what you wanted. This is why you booked me."

He squirmed where he lay. I repositioned myself so that I was straddling him. He wasn't getting away this time. I felt his hands relax. I did the same with mine. I was relieved that he didn't try and pull away from me. Feeling more confident, I moved my hands away completely. Didn't touch him. Let him get used to this first. Let him get comfortable with this. One slow step at a time.

"Do most men do this?" he asked.

⚔

I told the man - a polite man in his late forties - to lie down in the bath. He didn't need telling twice. The excitement on his face amazed me. I waited a moment for him to get comfortable before I climbed in. I didn't lie down. I remained in a squat position above his face. I felt his tongue against my pussy. The way it flicked across my clit - clearly a man who knew what he was doing.

"Wait a minute," I told him.

I couldn't do it whilst he was licking me. I needed to concentrate. Everything about what we were doing felt unnatural to me. It felt wrong. A little bit exciting but definitely wrong. Couldn't let him down. It was on the list of services I offered so I couldn't let him down. It would invariably lead to negative feedback. They ask for it, they get it. Those were my own rules - so long as what is wanted is on my list of services anyway.

"Do it," he murmured.

He sounded desperate but try as I might - I couldn't do what was being asked of me. I leaned across and took a hold of his cock in my hands. I couldn't believe how hard it was and I hadn't even started yet. The anticipation for what was to come, no doubt. He sighed as I started to wank him. I leaned further forward and put him in my mouth. I closed my eyes and continued to concentrate and then it happened. A trickle first and then a steady stream. I felt his tongue against me as I continued to urinate over his face as he had asked in his initial booking request. A Golden Shower, he called it. The money was good; an extra fifty pounds. And I told him we'd have to do it in the bath which he was fine with.

"Give it to me!" he begged between each sodden flick of his tongue.

He sighed out loud and I felt that familiar twitch from his penis between my lips. Before I had a chance to react he was shooting jet after jet of hot semen to the back of my throat where I expertly swallowed it down.

He had paid for an hour, plus the additional fifty pounds.

We had been fifteen minutes.

⚔

"That's another question."

I undid his belt buckle and pulled at his belt until it came free from his trousers. I threw it over my shoulder where it fell to the floor.

"Not all men need as much encouragement as you," I told him. "Some can't wait to get started. Some have even started before we're out of the hallway, despite the fact they haven't paid for the session yet."

All the time I was talking to him I noticed that he couldn't keep his eyes off my breasts - which he still held on to, gently squeezing periodically. I took the opportunity to try and get him in the mood for more than just a grope.

"Most men like similar things though. They like to feel my lips around their cocks. They like to feel me gently sucking on them. The feel of my tongue flicking against their heads. My hands running over their bodies. Caressing their balls, stroking their inner thighs. The feel of my wet, tight cunt sliding down their hard erections or rubbing over their faces as they greedily lap my tasty juices. Some men like to be tied down so that they're completely helpless. My prisoner to do with as I see fit…"

I put my hands on his chest and started rocking backwards and forward with each suggestion as to what previous clients liked. Jon closed his eyes and tilted his head back and I could feel him harden beneath me. He sighed with pleasure.

"What are you thinking about?" I purred as I continued rocking. "Are you wondering what it's like to slide inside of me? Are you wondering what it feels like? The tightness of it? The wetness?"

I started to moan as though it were already inside me as I continued rocking on top of him. I never usually feel the need to moan when having sex. I'd breathe heavily but rarely moan. The men that pay for it though - they like to hear the moans and groans. The porn-star noises, as I like to refer to them. It makes them feel as though they're doing a good job when - nine times out of ten - they're not even close to hitting the right spot. Jon started to moan too as I worked his cock through his jeans.

"Or maybe you'd rather I took you in your mouth? Suck you nice and deep. Slowly…"

I sighed as I continued to writhe on top of him.

"Wait!"

He sat up and pushed me off him with a strong shove. I fell to the side and he jumped up off the bed and onto his feet.

"I'm sorry," he said.

"What is wrong with you?"

I got off the bed too as he started to gather up the clothes he had taken off; belt and shirt. He put his shirt on first.

"I made a mistake. I shouldn't have come here. I really am sorry."

"What are you talking about? It looked like you were enjoying it from where I was sitting."

He started to put his belt on.

"Just wait a minute," I said.

I blocked the doorway to stop him from leaving. If he really didn't want an appointment with me then I'd let him leave. I certainly wasn't about to force him to do something he didn't want to do but I needed to know what his problem was. I needed to know why he kept stopping himself from just going with the flow and allowing himself the joy on offer.

"What did I do that was so wrong?" I asked him. "One minute you seemed to be getting into it and the next - this. What happened? I mean, if you don't want the appointment, that is fine but at least let me know why."

"It's not you, it's me…" he said.

"Really?!"

I couldn't believe he was using that line on me. Especially given the fact we weren't even a couple that were breaking up. I was the whore, he was the client. Nothing more and nothing less.

I pushed him, "I'm not letting you go until you talk to me. You need to leave me knowing what is going on. Do that - and you can have your money back and leave. We'll say no more about it. But if you go - without telling me - I'm keeping the money and I promise you this, I will not see you again. No more apologies via email, no more repeat bookings… Honey, I'm the best in the area and I'm offering you the time of your life for an appointment you have already paid for. What's the problem?"

I knew I was ranting but I couldn't help myself. Years in the profession and this was the first time I had been in this position. It felt weird. Alien. Horrible.

"I'm just nervous," he said, "it feels strange to be standing here with you."

⋏

"I've never been with a girl before."

"You're a virgin? That's fine, sweetie…"

"No, that's not what I meant. I've never been with a hooker before. Hooker. Is that even the right term? That's not offensive, is it?"

The man standing with me in the bedroom was a bumbling wreck of nerves. It was both sweet and pathetic at the same time. Not used to seeing men like this but I didn't show my real feelings. I show an understanding. The money part had been taken care of already. Just as I had done so on all my appointments, I had taken care of it downstairs in the hallway before leading the man up here.

"Hooker is fine," I reassured him.

I had offered him a drink, downstairs, but he had declined. I offered him a seat on the edge of the bed which he accepted. I sat with him. Our bodies were touching. An early trick I learned; touch makes people feel more comfortable.

"So I'm your first working girl then?" I asked.

"Working girl? Is that the term you prefer?"

"Honestly, I don't mind what you call me. It's fine. Well - within reason," I laughed. "What made you choose me?" I asked him.

He blushed, "You looked pretty."

"Thank you. Not so bad yourself."

A cliche of a line but it works nevertheless.

"Well look - we'll take things nice and slowly. How about we start with a nice massage?"

"Sure," he smiled.

Ryan was his name. A man in his fifties, if I had to guess. I found it hard to believe I was his first working girl. Usually guys start off young and just continue seeing them throughout their lives. It was rare just to find someone who woke up one day and decided to book a lady of the night.

"Take your clothes off," I instructed him.

"Really?" he seemed nervous.

"Relax. You're in good hands. Nothing I haven't seen before."

I gave him a cheeky wink.

"If it makes you feel better, I'll even turn around."

I stood up and turned my back on him. I listened as he took the opportunity to stand up too before he started to undress. Less than a couple of minutes later and I heard the bed springs squeak as he climbed into the bed.

"Am I safe to turn around?" I asked.

I didn't wait for an answer.

Ryan was lying on his front. I straddled him so that I could give him a nice back massage.

"You realise these are going to have to come off at some point!" I said.

He was still wearing his underwear. He wasn't the first man to leave them on until the last possible minute - almost as though they were embarrassed to be completely naked in front of me. Funny really. I'm not sure how they think these appointments work. They could stay on for now whilst I give him a little back rub; just a little something to help him relax into the session.

"You're good at this," he said, enjoying my touch as I rubbed his shoulders.

"Well don't get too comfortable," I told him, "your turn next!"

I give them a nice massage to make them feel more relaxed. I then strip off and allow them to massage me. It's not long before their mind turns to a more intimate of touches. They usually start by rubbing my shoulders but soon their hands are all over my arse and then - before you know it - I'm told to roll onto my back and their hands are running over my breasts and between my legs. It's at that moment I reach down to touch them too and we move onto the next stage; the blow job. Yes the massage relaxes them but - more importantly - it moves things along.

$$\blacktriangle$$

"I promise you, you're in good hands. Just sit with me. We don't have to do anything. We can just talk if that's what you really want. You've paid for my time, you might as well use it up."

Jon froze.

"We can just talk?"

"Sure."

"Okay."

"And then - if you feel like it - I can give you a nice massage."

Moment of truth. I moved away from the doorway. I half expected him to make a run for the door but he didn't. I slid my dressing gown over my shoulders, having taken it from the door, and walked back over to the bed and sat on the edge of it. He didn't move. He just stood there. I patted the edge of the mattress next to where I was sitting. He came over and sat with me.

"Are you sure I can't get you a drink?" I asked.

"Maybe a water?"

"Coming right up! And when I get back - you can tell me what's going on."

I climbed off the bed and left the room, leaving him to it. As I headed down the stairs I couldn't help but wonder if he was turning into the type of client I had seen so many times before; the ones who believed they could save me from what I do. It would certainly explain all the questions; my relationship status, whether I feel safe, what I have to do for the money... Soon he'd be telling me I could stop what I was doing and that he'd be there to support me. It was all starting to make perfect sense. He doesn't want to touch me as a prostitute because he wants to touch me as a partner.

Pretty Woman Syndrome before he even had me?

That one was new.

⅄

I poured out two glasses of the red wine the client had brought with him and walked with them through to the bedroom where he was waiting for me. He had already taken his clothes off and made himself comfortable on the bed. A younger gentleman of about twenty-three years old. Richard. He had come to the house with a stack of money, a large bouquet of flowers and - so he says - one of the best bottles of red money can buy. The flowers looked as though they came from a petrol station and the bottle of red was the kind you'd usually find in a supermarket deal offering three bottles for a tenner. I acted suitably impressed and even pretended the drink was nice when I took a swig from it.

"Nice, isn't it?" he asked as he took a swig too.

He swirled the liquid around his mouth, as though at a fancy wine tasting event, and swallowed it loudly. I knew what he was trying to do. I had seen it before. Little did he know - though - was that I had seen it done so much better than he was trying. The 'pricey' flowers, the 'expensive' bottle of red - the fact he showed up in a 'posh' suit - he was pretending to be something he wasn't. He handed the money over as though it were nothing to him but I'd wager that it was a lot more than he could realistically afford.

"If this goes well," he said after another mouthful, "fancy making this a daily appointment?"

I had a bet with myself that if I were to root through his wallet I'd find a student id card.

"Mmmm. That would be nice."

Soon he'd be asking for discount, next he'd be expecting freebies. Before you know it - he'd be wanting to call me his girlfriend, make me stop seeing other men and fabricate some wedding plans. It was always the same from clients who came here looking to impress me. They wanted more than a prostitute. They wanted a trophy. Like it's some kind of conquest to win the 'love' of a whore. We see so many men, yet this one man was good enough to make us love them out of all others. It was pathetic but it was also a common occurrence - at least once a month. I much preferred the clients who came here just looking to have an orgasm. They were simple.

"Of course we'll negotiate the rates, yeah?"

Bingo.

First comes discount, then comes freebies.

I took his drink off him and put it to the side with my own glass. Before he had a chance to ask what I was doing I started to french kiss him. My tongue tenderly stroking his. Anything to shut him up.

"What are you doing?" I asked Jon.

I was standing in the bedroom doorway with his glass of water that he'd requested. I had been there for a couple of minutes, watching him as he went through my drawers. He jumped at the sound of my voice.

"I said, what are you doing?"

I set his glass to one side.

"I think you should leave," I told him.

"It's not what it looks like," he said.

He looked embarrassed and shifted awkwardly.

"It looks like you were going through my stuff."

"Okay, it's a little like it looks."

"There's nothing in here to rob."

"I wasn't robbing you."

"You were going through my stuff. If you weren't robbing me, what the hell were you doing?"

"I was just trying to get to know you."

"By going through my things?"

He didn't say anything. He was just standing there with a sheepish expression on his face. The funny thing was - I actually believed what he was saying. I had had people try and rob me in the past - one of them even succeeded in getting away with it - and when I confronted them they all got aggressive in their defiance. He was just looking stupid.

"Asking questions isn't enough for you?" I asked him.

I picked the glass of water up and handed it over to him. He took it with thanks. I walked around him and sat on the edge of the bed. I don't know what it is about him which makes me feel sorry for him - protective almost. The first client to get under my skin and I barely knew him.

"I'm sorry. I really wasn't trying to steal anything."

"So you want to get to know me?" I asked him.

He nodded.

"Why?"

"Find you interesting. What you do."

"Writing a story on prostitutes?" I asked.

He shook his head.

"No. Promise."

"Do this with other girls?"

He shook his head again.

"I've asked a lot of questions. Want me to start taking items of clothing off?" I asked, a smile on my face.

He shook his head.

"May I sit down?"

I moved over on the bed making room for him to sit there with me. I didn't touch him. We sat there in silence for a moment. Neither one of us knew what to say.

"So what else do you want to know about me then?" I asked him.

"Does your family know what you do?"

BEFORE

Three more years have passed. A young girl has turned into a young woman. Fifteen years old now and fully aware of what was happening. The innocent party yet on the receiving end of her mother's blows. Slap after slap hitting her face. The taste of semen still fresh in her mouth. Called all the names under the sun except her own. Whore. Cunt. Slut. Of course the monster had vanished into the night air leaving nothing behind but a few personal possessions, a sticky residue and a promise to get someone to collect the rest of its stuff.

The mother stopped hitting the young lady long enough to grab the girl's school rucksack from where it hung over the back of the chair.

"It wasn't my fault!" the young woman cried.

The mother wasn't hearing her and - if she was - she was ignoring her as she started to throw socks and knickers into the bag, along with a few items of clothes she could squeeze in there. She zipped it shut and tossed it to her naked daughter.

"Get the fuck out of my house."

"What? No. Please. It wasn't my fault, mum! He made me do it!"

"I don't want to hear it! Get out!"

An over-reaction from a distraught parent who knew she'd not only been betrayed but also that she had failed her daughter. Out of sight, out of mind. Try and move on, try and pick up the pieces. Her head was all over the place. A banging sensation to the side of her temples. She needed to lie down. Needed a nap. Knew she wouldn't sleep. Never sleep again. Her daughter's face a reminder as to what she'd been blind to. For how long? How long had it been going on? Under her own roof.

"Get out!" she screamed again.

A mother turned her back on her daughter.

The young lady crawled from her bed and started to put some clothes on. Her hands shaking. Tears streaming down her face. Vagina aching from the monsters thrust. No one cared. She held out a hand to touch her mother's back; let her know she was there. Her mother shrugged it off.

"I want you out of here!" she hissed.

"I have no money. Where will I go?"

The mother tugged at the rings on her finger; one wedding band and one diamond engagement. She threw them at her daughter and spat that she should sell them.

"I don't want to go!" the young lady wept.

The mother shoved her hard. She fell backwards and out of the room. Her back slammed against the landing wall.

"Get out!" the mother yelled again.

"But where?"

"I want you to leave."

The young lady didn't move. She stormed over to her and grabbed her by the arm before leading her down the stairs towards the front door. The girl screamed that she didn't want to go anywhere, she had nowhere to go. She yelled that it wasn't her fault. She begged for forgiveness. Pleaded to be allowed to stay. The front door was opened and she was shoved out into the cold night. Before she could say anything else - the door was slammed in her face. She fell to her knees and screamed for her mum. Her mum didn't respond.

The monster did though, lurking in the shadows.

PART THREE

15 Years Later

Jon's question caught me by surprise. My customers had asked me many things during their visits but this was the first time anyone had ever brought my family into the appointment with them. Talking of them was as unwelcome to me as my general presence was to them. I tried to close my mind to the barrage of memories trying to flood their way back to the forefront of my mind with little success. Just answer his question and move on. Simple.

"I haven't spoken to anyone in my family for a number of years," I told Jon.

My answer surprised me just as much as the initial question itself. The first time I think I have ever been one hundred percent honest with a client. But was he a client? I'd taken his money - yes - but we hadn't done anything other than talk. Not really fair to label him the same as the others.

"Must be hard," he said.

He sounded genuinely sympathetic to my situation. I didn't ask for his sympathy though. I don't want to be seen as a victim. I chose this path for myself. I could have got out a long time ago but I felt as though it was my duty to do what I do. I'm not the victim. Maybe once but definitely not anymore. I refuse to be. The only victims around here are some of the men who come to see me. The ones who don't leave.

I couldn't believe how many men opted for this position; lying on his back with his cock pushed right to the back of my throat. Me sitting down on his face, his tongue buried deep within my vagina. His nose pushed up against my puckered asshole. I'd press all of my weight down on him and hold myself there, whilst he squirmed beneath me, until I felt he needed some more air. Then I'd sit up, long enough for him to gulp down some more oxygen, before pushing back down. All the punters loved it and never seemed to last long.

I felt the client's tongue slip from my ass as I moved off his face.

"So fucking good," he sighed, as I continued to suck him off. "I should pay you to teach my wife…"

I paused what I was doing for a split second.

"I didn't know you were married."

"Keep the ring in my pocket when I see ladies. Believe it or not, some of you actually have a fucking conscience. Not many, mind you. But some. Forget I said anything, slip of the tongue. Come on, don't stop."

He grabbed my hips and pulled me back down onto his face. As soon as he let go, I climbed off.

"What are you doing? Come on. I was enjoying that."

I turned round so that we were face to face and held my finger up to him. I waved it from side to side.

"Uh uh, I'm the one in charge here."

I jumped off the bed a moment and fetched a scarf from the cupboard.

"What's that for?" he asked.

I answered him with actions and tied his hands - by the wrists - to the headboard.

"Kinky," he laughed.

"I told you," I said, "I'm the one in charge here."

I climbed back onto the bed and straddled his face once more.

"Yes, ma'am."

His voice muffled as I lowered myself back onto his face. Immediately he started lapping at me with his wet tongue, enjoying the taste of what he believed to be my juices. Despite his best efforts, I was as dry as a bone. Only appeared wet thanks to the lubricant I applied before the appointment. I pressed down hard as I put him back into my mouth and resumed sucking.

The usual pattern was suck and toss for twenty seconds and then sit up for five. Sit back down again and suck and toss for another twenty. Another five off the face and back down again. I would continue with that pattern until I felt the sperm either hit the back of my throat or fill the condom - depending on whether I made them wear one or not. Always for penetration, sometimes for oral. Depended on the level of stink.

This was different though.

It had already been longer than twenty seconds and I was still pushing down hard on his face. His flicking tongue had definitely slowed. I couldn't help but wonder whether he realised he was suffocating yet or whether he simply didn't care; having far too much fun licking me out. All I could think about was the wife he had waiting for him at home. I wondered whether she knew what her partner was doing or whether she was blind to it. If she didn't know - what would she have thought had she found out? The guy was scum. Reminded me of my own father and how he destroyed my mother. How he destroyed me. Can't bear to think of this asshole doing the same thing to the woman he was supposed to love. The way I saw it - I was doing her a favour.

The client started banging on the headboard - no doubt trying to get my attention.

I looked back and saw that he was trying to pull at the scarf which had him bound. I had tied the knot pretty well but wasn't one hundred percent comfortable that it would hold. I took hold of his testicles and squeezed them as hard as I could. His hands clenched together as the pain became unbearable for him. I pushed down harder. I could feel him trying to get air from beneath me. No chance. I pushed down harder again, still crushing his balls. The more pain he was in - the less he fought against me. And then - with no warning - his body seemed to go limp beneath me. I looked back at his hands and they were motionless and seemingly relaxed. I didn't move. I stayed where I was. Didn't let off any pressure either. Kept it just the same. Had to be sure he was gone. I sat up - staying firmly pressed down where I was seated - and pressed my hand against his chest to see if I could feel his heart beating. I kept it there for about a minute. There was nothing. He was gone. Before I even realised what was happening, I found myself crying.

▲

"I'm sorry. I didn't mean to upset you."

I wiped a lone tear from my cheek with the back of my hand. All the thoughts buzzing around my head and it's the one of my parents that sticks. I wiped my hand on the duvet. I felt stupid. I didn't know what to say. I couldn't remember the last time someone saw my emotions. My real emotions, that is.

"I should go."

Jon went to get off the bed. I stopped him.

"It's fine. I was just being stupid."

He didn't look convinced.

"Come on," I pushed him, "what other questions do you have?"

He sat there a moment, staring into my eyes. He looked as though he was trying to work me out. He needed a lot more appointments before he'd come close to that.

"What do you do after your appointments?" he asked.

"What do you mean?"

"The rest of your days - what do you do when you're not servicing your clients?"

▲

I waited a moment more. Scared to get off. Scared to see what I had done. Can't delay it any longer though. I sat up and moved further down the bed. I sat on the edge, too nervous to look back at the corpse behind me. Can't delay though. Need to get up. Need to fix what I've done.

Fix what I've done? How do you fix something like this?

I slowly turned back around. The man was lying there. His face was staring up at the ceiling. His mouth was agape. His tongue hanging from the side. He was blue. I took hold of his foot and gave it a shake. Part of me hoped he'd suddenly take a breath and all would be okay in the world. He didn't. Dead as a doornail. I did this.

I got off the bed and walked to the other side of the room. I kept my back to him. I don't want to go to jail and yet that's exactly where I am going. You can't get away with murder. They lock you in a cell and throw away the key. Doesn't matter if you do think you were doing their partners a favour. Oh God, his wife. He has a wife. Children? A whole family or just a wife?

I looked around to his pile of clothes on the floor. I hurried towards them; picking up his trousers. A quick feel of his pockets and I found which one contained his wallet. Reaching in, I took it out and dropped the clothing back onto the floor. A medium sized gold band fell from one of the pockets and rolled under the bed. Ignore it. Turned my attention back to the wallet. Brown wallet. Leather. Stuffed with cash and card. Flipping it open revealed no family pictures. None of his wife, none of any potential children. I took the cash out and put it to the side before tossing the wallet onto the pile of clothes crumpled on the floor. Gaze went back to the body.

"Shit."

⋏

"You're a nosy one, aren't you?"

"I'm sorry."

"Stop apologising. It's fine. Can't remember the last time someone wanted to know about me. Usually I'm nothing but a walking, talking fuck toy."

"Don't say that…"

"It's true. It's fine. It's what I chose."

"Why did you choose it?" he asked.

A question that hit from out of the blue. Another question too personal to answer with the truth. I had answered him the previous day: Told him I had gotten used to the money despite only initially getting into the industry to pay my way through my degree. Was he testing me or did he forget we'd already spoken about that? I diverted back to his previous question.

"After an appointment I strip the bed down and have a bath. I'll check my emails for further bookings and I'll start to get some dinner ready, I guess."

The truth.

Sort of.

Other appointments saw me dragging the bodies from bedroom to bathroom. I'd have to keep stopping on the way because I'd get tired. Some of the men were light, some were heavy. I remember the first client - the one who suggested hiring me to teach his wife - he was definitely on the heavy side. I wouldn't quit though. I couldn't. I got him - and the others - into the bathroom and I managed to get them into the bath itself. Easiest way to contain the mess. Not that there was any mess when I killed the first man. Not for the first few days anyway. I left him in the bath for a while whilst I plucked up the courage to do what needed to be done. Didn't see any clients. I just shut myself in the house for a few days convinced I was going to go to prison. That the police were going to come for me at any moment.

No one came though.

I drove his car from my drive and abandoned it miles away on a dirt track I found weaving through a wooded area. Just left it there with the keys in it after wiping down the surfaces with my scarf. I guessed that's what was supposed to be done. I didn't know for sure. Didn't see any harm in following through with the action anyway.

"That's it?" Jon asked.

I smiled.

"That's it."

"Oh."

"What did you expect?"

He shrugged.

"I don't know. I just thought there might have been a little more to…"

"…My life?"

He nodded.

i was puzzled by what he meant but didn't ask him to explain further.

"I'm happy," I told him.

"You are?"

I nodded. He smiled. Seemed genuinely happy by what I said. Without a word he downed his glass of water and stood up. He handed me the glass. I took it from him.

"Thank you."

"Going somewhere?"

"Been an hour already," he said.

He actually looked a little disappointed. I patted the side of the bed.

"It's fine. Sit down."

"What?"

"I said, sit."

He did as I told him and sat back down.

"You're sure?"

"I don't have anything else planned for the day," I told him, "and I probably owe you a little extra after yesterday. But don't tell anyone else."

I used the previous shortened appointment as an excuse but the truth was - I actually liked him sitting here with me. There was something about him. His presence. It calmed me. It made me feel... Normal. I couldn't remember the last time I felt such feelings. It was nice.

"Well as long as you're sure. I don't want to be in the way."

"You're not. I'd say if you were. It's fine."

"Well... Thank you. Very generous and unexpected."

I stood up.

"You know what? I'm hungry. If you don't want anything else - can I at least offer you a sandwich?" I asked.

He smiled.

"I'd love one. Thank you."

"You're very well spoken. Has anyone ever told you that?"

I met a lot of people in this line of work. A lot of them were well spoken but they also carried an air of confidence about them. One which suggested a private education - although not necessarily the case. They weren't usually this well spoken and this quiet and shy. I didn't know what to make of it. It was nice, yes, but it also seemed out of place.

"My mum and dad died," he said. "Foster parents raised me. I guess I picked it up from them."

I was a little taken aback by his honesty. He could have said anything. He could have even used the private education card - even if it weren't the truth. I wasn't sure what to say exactly not that he looked like he needed me to say anything.

"I'm sorry to hear about your mum and dad," I said after a slight delay.

He shrugged it off and stood up.

"Can I help you with the sandwiches?" he asked.

"Yeah. Sure. You can butter the bread…"

I took his hand and led him down the stairs towards the kitchen, having tightened my dressing gown. Not the first time I had led a client to the kitchen in such a manner - although, slight difference the last time I took a man down… I hadn't been holding him by his hand.

The client was grinning like an idiot as we made our way down the stairs, me leading him with my hand wrapped around his cock as though it were a leash. Although he wasn't new to the world of paying for sex, this was completely new to him. Long term fantasy lived - for many years - in his head, finally about to come true. All I could think was thank God this was his house. His house, his mess.

We walked into the kitchen. He had been a busy man. The sides were lined with various foods. There were bowls of jelly, custard and even beans swimming in tomato sauce. I also couldn't help but notice a couple of cream based cakes too. Plastic sheeting covered the floor and nearly tripped me as I entered the kitchen in my high heels.

My first experience of sploshing. An act which would see us get down and dirty with the foods on offer. I turned to the client.

"So where do we start?" I asked him.

He'd already told me in his email that he was happy to take the lead when I replied to him saying I didn't have experience with this side of the industry.

"Always with something savoury," he said, still grinning. "End with the sweet stuff."

"Beans it is."

"What's so funny?" Jon asked as we walked through to the kitchen.

"Just smiling," I said.

There was no need to lie to him. Yes he was a client but he wasn't like the others. I figured there was no harm in telling him.

"Okay, it's just the last time I led a client to the kitchen it was for a different kind of act…"

He stopped me, "Is that all I am to you? A client?"

I didn't know what to say. Did he think, because I had allowed him to stay a little longer, that he was more than just a client? Was it what I was thinking earlier? He was trying to pretend to be something he wasn't so that he could get close to me and try and 'win me round'? Become my boyfriend? Pretty Woman Syndrome without even the need to have his cock inside of me? Unusual but possible. It's just - they normally like to test the wares first.

I corrected myself, "Sorry. I meant to say - the last time I took anyone to the kitchen."

"What is sploshing?"

He asked the question within a split second of me explaining what I meant - as though the answer wasn't even that important to him in the first place.

"Throwing food over each other, tipping custard and such down into our underwear and rubbing each other…"

"Sounds weird."

I laughed, "Sexy to some, weird to others. I have to confess, it wasn't for me."

"Don't you sometimes think you're worth more than all of this?"

His question took me by surprise - not for the first time. A suggestion in his tone that what I did was lowly. I guess it was. I had certainly felt dirty the first time I slept with a client. At least I did after the initial joy of earning the money. A joy which lasted for about as long as it took to spend the cash which - with all my debt - wasn't long.

"Sorry I didn't mean how that sounded. It's just…" he stopped himself from talking and I didn't encourage him to continue. Some things were best left unsaid.

I changed the subject, "I'm not sure what I have in the cupboards. I definitely have ham and cheese. How does that sound?"

"Sounds lovely."

I opened the fridge and took out the ham and cheese. I handed it to him and he put it on the side. I took out the butter and walked with it over to the bread bin and took that out too. I pulled out a handful of slices of bread and put them on the side. The lid off the butter, a knife from the cutlery drawer.

"Did you want me to do that?" Jon offered.

I shook my head.

"Won't take me long."

I took a second knife from the cutlery drawer and handed it to him. The first time I had ever offered a client a sharp object. Usually I try and keep them out of the way - just in case they're damaged in the head. Jon took the knife from me and paused a moment - as did I. Had I made a mistake?

"I thought you said no."

"What?"

"Buttering the bread. Thought you said it wouldn't take you long? I mean it's fine but... Just confused."

"Oh. Sorry. No. I mean yes. I can do the bread. That's for the cheese. If you could cut some thin slices. That'd be useful."

"Sure."

I watched as Jon started to slice through the cheese with the knife.

"Not too thick," I told him.

He adjusted his technique resulting in thinner slices. I turned my attention back to the bread. Knife in hand, I started to butter it.

I screamed out of both frustration and desperation. This fucking knife. It cut through the client's skin with ease, struggled a little with the muscle and wasn't making even a dent in his bones. I threw the bloodied knife across the room. It landed with a thud and slid into the corner of the tiled bathroom.

I burst into tears again as the weight of my actions landed heavily upon me. He came here alive and now he's dead. He's dead because of me. My reasons for killing him didn't matter anymore. All I could think about was the fact he used to be a human. A man - of sorts. And now he was just a festering corpse who'd been stinking out my bathroom for the last couple of days.

I stormed out of the room and slammed the door shut. Out of sight out of mind. But he's not though. He's still there. I can't leave him here. Need to accept more bookings on an incall basis and can't do it with him stinking the house out. I hurried down the stairs - not a run but not a dawdle - and out into the garage. A few tools had been left in here. Not sure whether they belonged to another previous tenant or whether the owner of the house left them there to be helpful to people moving in. A hammer, a spanner, some blunted screwdrivers and a rusty saw. I pulled it from the shelf, knocking the screwdrivers crashing to the concrete floor, and touched the blade. It wasn't razor sharp but hopefully it would do the job.

I took it back up to the bathroom. When I opened the door, he was there taunting me with his vacant stare. I could almost hear him laughing. Fuck you. I walked over to the bath and leaned in, saw in hand. I started on his arm. The combination of both the scent and sound of saw teeth grinding through bone made me gag. A second later and I threw up over the client. Some would have paid good money for that. I spat the remainder of the sick from my mouth and continued to saw with increased effort. I could feel it was having the desired effect and just wanted to get it over and done with before trying to think about what to do with the bits I'd cut away. Couldn't help but think I should have thought this through properly before suffocating him. Thought this through properly? I hadn't given it any thought. Stupid. I kept trying to force my mind back to why I had killed him, to try and make the act of disposal a little easier on myself. I did it for his wife. I did it for the lady at home who was unaware her husband was a cheating asshole. She'd just think he went missing. They'd find the car but not the body. Sure she might pine after him but at least he has died with her loving him. In time she will get over it. When a man cheats on a woman so badly though - it's harder to get over. The feeling of abandonment. The feeling he doesn't want you. My mother didn't get over it. At least with him missing - she still gets to believe her vows meant something to him. She wouldn't sit there feeling as though she'd wasted so many years of her life. I saved her. She just doesn't know it. As the saw cut through the final piece of his bone the thought was clear in my head; I did this for her.

I wiped the sweat from my brow with a bloodied hand before taking a deep breath and starting on the next limb. I wish there were a quicker way.

⋏

Jon layered the cheese into the sandwich, on top of the ham, and stepped to one side so that I could cut it with the knife I'd been using to spread the butter. Probably would have been better to use a sharper knife but I'm used to using substandard tools. You'd think I'd learn by now.

"Triangles!" Jon pointed out.

He laughed.

"Best way to make a sandwich. My mum taught me that. Somehow they taste better than when you cut them into rectangles…"

Jon smiled. I realised I had made a mistake by bringing her back into the conversation. It was only a matter of time before…

"So why don't you talk to your family anymore?" he asked.

… And that was what I was afraid of. More personal questions.

I took a bite of my sandwich to buy myself a little time to think of a suitable reason why I wouldn't be talking to my family, without the need to actually give him the truth.

B E F O R E

Young lady trapped in the small flat. Only allowed out with the monster by her side. A threat that if she spoke about that which took place behind closed doors she'd live to regret it. A promise that - if she played nice, he'd play nice. The knock at the door echoed around the small apartment but she didn't dare move from where she lay. A state of undress she didn't want others to see her in.

The monster stepped into a pair of trousers and pulled them up. Another knock at the door as he made his way down the hallway towards the front door. The young lady was curious as to who it was. They didn't have guests come to the house, especially not those who were uninvited.

"What are you doing here?"

The young lady moved from bed to door, keeping out of sight, and strained to hear what was being discussed. She recognised the voice speaking to the monster, she knew she did, but she couldn't place who it belonged to. Definitely someone she knew though. Words merged into nothing more than a sound. Too faint to make out properly although the tone was filled - at first - with regret and sorry before turning to one of anger and hostility. Shouting and swearing now, easy to make out what was going on.

"It's not my fault!" the monster yelled back.

The young lady stepped into the hallway after wrapping a dressing gown around her naked form. Two men standing by the door; one was the monster and one was someone she thought she recognised from a party from years gone by. The man spotted the girl. A look of sadness on his face and then - as before - anger. He turned back to the monster.

"She's with you? We've been looking for her!"

"Not very hard. Been with me since her mother kicked her out!"

"You sick son of a bitch!" he swung his fist at the monster and smiled when it connected with it's face.

The monster turned with the force of the smack and noticed the young lady watching in fright.

"Go back inside your bedroom, sweetie."

He didn't ask again. He turned back to the man who'd struck him.

"I suggest you leave."

"Are you going to tell her?" the man demanded. A slight pause before he questioned him further, "What the fuck is the matter with you? You're sick."

"Fuck you."

"She didn't want us to call the police. Was scared of the neighbours and town gossips finding out but I guess it doesn't matter what she wants anymore..."

"Fuck you!" the monster yelled again.

The young lady didn't see anything from where she cowered in the room. She wanted to run to the stranger. She wanted him to take her away from it all; give her a new life. She didn't dare run to him though and even if she had - had she been able to see down the hallway, she'd see the man shoved from the doorway and back into the hallway of the apartment block they were staying in.

She'd have seen the door slam shut as opposed to just hearing it.

As the monster's footsteps walked down the hallway, back towards the room, the young lady jumped back onto the bed and curled herself into a little ball. The monster stepped into the room and walked over to the bed. He paused there. She didn't look. She didn't even look when he sat on the edge of the bed. Had she done so, she'd have seen the monster had it's back to her.

"Your mother's dead," he said.

The young lady wanted to cry but didn't dare.

Can't anger the monster. It only makes it rougher.

PART FOUR

15 YEARS LATER

<u>A Two Way Conversation</u>

I kept Jon's answer short and sweet despite the urge to completely ignore the question about my lack of contact with my family. My family? They aren't my family. They haven't been for at least fifteen years, maybe longer. She's dead. He's... Gone. I don't know where and, more to the point, I don't care.

"Just lost contact with them," I said.

"Do you miss them?" he asked.

"Do you mind if we talk about something else?" I asked.

"I'm sorry. I didn't mean to pry. I was just interested."

"I don't mind answering your questions, if that's what you really want from me, but let's keep questions of that nature out of it, okay?"

He nodded and took a bite from his sandwich.

"You're right," he said with a mouthful, "it does taste better as triangles."

I smiled before tipping my own sandwiches into the bin. Funny how talk of my lost family can snatch away my appetite. I shut the lid of the bin. Certainly easier than disposing of body parts.

⚔

The toilet water flooded over the bowl and spilled its reddish colour over the floor.

"Shit!"

I backed up to avoid getting any of it onto my feet. Pointless really considering how much gore I have over myself after all the cutting. I gagged, a common occurrence now, as I reached my hand back into the toilet bowl and fished the man's wrist from the u-bend.

Stupid.

⋏

"You aren't hungry?" he asked. His eyes fixed on the bin where I'd dropped my sandwiches.

"Must have gone past it," I said. "Happens sometimes when I leave it too long."

"I'm sorry. I didn't mean to keep you from eating."

"My fault. I should have got myself some breakfast before you came. I don't usually have lunch so late."

He continued eating his sandwich. For the first time in his company, I found myself feeling uncomfortable. His eyes fixed upon me. I tried to avert his attention.

"What about you?" I asked him.

He frowned, "What about me?"

"What's your story?" I asked.

"Well you already know about my parents," he said, "and my foster parents were nice enough to me..."

"Not all of that. You today. Who you are today. You know what I do but I have no idea what you do."

"What I do?"

"For a living?"

"Oh. Right. Yes. Banks."

"You do banks?"

"Sorry. Banker. I'm a banker."

"Oh? Very fancy."

"I'm on the front desk. Help people with their withdrawals, transfers, complaints... That kind of things. Nothing fancy about it. Bottom rung of the ladder type of thing."

"Oh. Well. Good place to start. Work your way up."

He looked over my shoulder towards the garden outside. The perks of renting a house in the middle of nowhere; it afforded the privacy of a large garden. No neighbours beyond the trees lining it but - if there were any - they wouldn't be able to see into my house. More importantly they wouldn't be able to see into the garden either.

⅄

I threw the shovel onto the grass. Sweat dripped from my forehead and had been doing so long before I started digging the hole. Carrying the bags down from the bathroom was enough to see to that.

I looked at the hole. I'm not sure how deep it should be but it looks plenty deep enough now. I hoped it was anyway. I dragged the first of the bags over to the hole and kicked it in. It landed with a thud. It wasn't long before the rest of the bags were with it. Couldn't believe I hadn't done this from the start. I had no plans to move from the house anytime soon, if ever, and I hadn't heard from the landlord for as long as I could remember. I kept the payments up on the rent and he left me to my own devices.

I reached down for the shovel and started to cover the bags with the freshly dug earth, the promise of a bath screaming to me. At least - screaming to me after I had cleaned it out.

⅄

"It's nice in the Summer," I agreed. "So what else is there then? There must be more to you than working in a bank."

"My life is pretty boring," he said.

"So that's why you came to see me? See how the other half live?"

He smiled.

"A little bit of excitement?" I pushed.

I walked over to him and stood close so that our bodies were almost touching.

"Could make it a lot more exciting for you," I laughed.

He put his hands up, "Okay, okay, what else do you want to know?"

"Nothing in particular," I said, "just be nice to get to know you. You know me. It's only fair that I know you."

"Well okay then. Worked at the bank for about…"

"Not the bank. You. Not what you do to make a living. What you do when you go home at night. That's the person I want to know."

"Really don't know what to say," he said.

I couldn't believe how shy he was about talking about himself. I couldn't decide whether it was a shyness or whether he was trying to hide something from me. Or was he just embarrassed and lacking in social skills? The fact he so easily blurted out that his parents were dead when I hadn't really asked… Definitely lacking social skills.

"So I live at home with my girlfriend… Been living together for about a year now…"

"Girlfriend?"

He nodded.

"You have a girlfriend?"

᛭

The man was screaming and pulling at the restraints that bound him to my bed. I couldn't help but laugh at him. He looked pathetic, this supposedly powerful man who crossed over my threshold with such confidence. Now look at him. Pathetic.

"You won't get away with this."

He kept saying the same thing again and again. A sense of urgency about his voice no doubt brought about by the touch of garden shears against his balls.

"I will get away with it," I told him. "I have got away with it. More than once. In fact, I think I've pretty much lost count the number of times I have got away with it…."

"Why? Why are you doing this? I brought you flowers!"

He did. Like so many clients before him - he did bring me flowers. And - like so many clients before him - they were purchased directly from the nearby petrol station. Cheap and most likely dead within the next twenty-four hours. A little like the client lying before me.

The appointment was going well enough. He was polite. He was a good lover. He paid without the need to be asked. But then it went downhill and fast.

Shot his load and started to spill his guts like they usually did in a post-coital cuddle. He started telling me about his woes at home; his wife in particular. She was a moaning hag, apparently. Don't think I've ever heard the word 'hag' before now. It just made him sound more pathetic. I told him I could make him forget all about his wife at home. He told me that I already had until I pointed out that he had been talking about her from the moment he ejaculated. I told him to lay back and close his eyes as I climbed from the bed to reach for the trusty restraints that I'd used so many times before.

"You have a wife," I reminded him.

"Yeah? So?"

"You ever think how she would feel if she found out you were here fucking me? Did that ever cross your mind?"

"So what?"

"My dad was like you," I hissed.

"Your dad fucked whores? So what? Loads of people do it…"

"And they can - but not whilst they're supposed to be in a loving relationship… It's not right…"

"You're a whore with fucking morals?!"

Keeping one hand on the shears - pressed against his testicles - I used the other hand to slap him in the face.

"Have some respect."

"For you? A fucking whore?"

I opened the shears up so that his bollocks were between the two blades.

"Do you want to say that again?"

"I'm sorry! I'm sorry! Please - just let me go…"

I continued with my story, "My dad cheated on my mum. It destroyed her world. The betrayal she felt - she never recovered from it. Do you know what she did?"

"Forgave him? Turned a blind eye? Realised which side her bread was buttered on?"

I sighed.

"She killed herself."

"That's not my fault!"

"What do you think your wife would do it she knew you were here?" I asked him.

"She'd forgive me. She loves me."

"Really? You're sure about that?"

"Yes. She's forgiven me before."

"Then she is an idiot."

I closed the shear's blades together until either side met in the middle. The man screamed the highest-pitched scream I had ever heard as his testicles rolled from the top of the shears and onto the bed next to him. I laughed at his pain.

"She'll do so much better without you," I yelled over the sounds of his scream.

I won't finish him off. I'll let him bleed out. I'll let him suffer. His wife has suffered. Only fair that he does. Going by the blood spilling from him, it won't take long. By the end of the day he'll be in a hole and his wife will be freed.

⋏

"You're surprised I have a girlfriend?" Jon asked.

"Well - honestly - yes. I thought you were a virgin and that's why you were scared of the intimacy I offered."

"A virgin?" he laughed. "No. Not a virgin. We've been together for a few years now. Moved in together about a year ago. It's nice…"

"Then if it's nice - why are you here?"

He hesitated a moment.

"Testing myself?"

"Testing yourself?"

"Yes."

"Don't follow."

I felt my feelings change towards him from the moment he said the word 'girlfriend'. Before that I not only pitied him a little bit but was actually starting to like him. He seemed like a decent bloke. He seemed genuine. Not sure if I have seen many of those in my life thinking back. The ones who see me, without a girl waiting for them at home, are hardly pillars of society. They have their se-crets; their skeletons hanging in the closet. And before these men - the ones who pay me for sex - there was only the monster that ruined my life. Not much of a role-model for future men to live up to. Jon was the closest I had got to finding someone 'normal'. I'm not saying I would have set up home with him but it was certainly a breath of fresh air. It was nice. Now I just felt sick to my stomach.

He was stuttering. I could see he was trying to back peddle. Trying to think of a way out of what he had said.

"What do you mean?" I pushed him.

"Well if I saw you and was able to sleep with you," he said, "then I guess my relationship wasn't as strong as I thought. I was thinking about proposing, you see. If I could have gone ahead with the appointment - well - guess she isn't the one and I'd be better off moving out and letting her find someone more deserving."

He was lying. I could see it in his face. There was something else. Something he was hiding.

He continued, "I was relieved when I went home yesterday. I mean - I felt bad for the way I ran out but the fact I didn't go through with the appointment... I was relieved."

"But you came back today."

He hesitated again. I could see the clogs working as he tried to figure out what to say to me.

"I felt like I needed to apologise to you," he said after a lengthy pause.

I'll tell you what happened. He had a taste for what I could offer but was too scared to go through with it yesterday. Temptation brought him back here. I couldn't help but wonder whether he was going to be like most of the other cheating men out there or whether he was going to run away again - back to the woman he was supposed to love. A test then...

"I don't believe you..." I said.

"I'm sorry?"

"I don't believe you. Why you came back today."

"Not sure I understand..."

I cut him off, "You came back today because, despite what you think you know of yourself, you want me to touch you."

I reached down and started stroking at his cock, through his trousers.

"You want to feel the tight, wet snatch of another woman…"

He pulled away from me after a slight hesitation which spoke volumes. He had inadvertently backed himself into the corner of the room though. No running out this time. I backed him against the wall as I continued to caress his genitals.

"Don't pretend you don't want it," I breathed heavily in his ear. I could hear that he was enjoying my touch. "Don't pretend you don't want me."

"Please stop…" he sighed.

His body betrayed his own words. He was hard at my touch. His hands were at his side. If he really wanted me to stop, he could have quite easily made me. I pulled at his belt, undoing it, and slid my hands down into his pants. My fingers wrapped around his erection. His sighs grew louder as his erection continued to harden until it was solid as a rock.

If he stops me… If he pushes me away… He has a chance… He can go home, never come back. He can live with his girlfriend. He can continue to live his life with her. With the woman he supposedly loves. If he doesn't stop me though, if he continues to enjoy my touch - I'll have no choice but to set his so-called love free. As I continued to tug him, with a firm grip, he continued to sigh. He even closed his eyes as though it helped take him to a special place where he could fully enjoy the sensations of my well-practised shake.

"How do you know if you really love your lady if you do not experience the love of another woman first? Talking to a woman isn't a test for you. Feeling the touch of a woman is. Letting the woman make you cum… Only then can you go home and know that the lady you have waiting for you is enough for you… Is all that you want for the rest of your life. Just you and her."

I increased rhythm.

"Do you want me to make you cum?" I asked.

"Please stop."

I didn't stop and neither did he try and stop me.

"How do you want me to make you cum?" I asked.

He didn't answer.

"With my hand like this? Or with my mouth? My tongue licking you? My mouth sucking you? My tight, wet pussy? You can go bareback if you want? Really feel how wet I am for you?"

He sighed harder. Clearly my words were leading him to the point of no return, along with my touch.

☖

The client's moans grew louder as he neared the orgasm he had paid for. I sat up, letting him slide out of me, and grabbed a hold of his dick with my left hand. My right pulled the rubber from his cock and tossed it to the floor. I quickly started wanking him before he lost the momentum we had built up.

"Does your wife touch you like this?" I asked. "Does she fuck you like I fuck you?"

I swapped hands. Left hand became free. Right hand around his cock. Keep momentum.

"Do you think she'd get off on watching us together?" I asked.

I looked at his face. He wasn't looking at me. Head tilted back. Body writhing around me. He wasn't even listening to the words I said. Not all of them anyway. He only heard the seductive tone that I used and picked out the odd words; namely fuck and touch. A test, then.

"Do you think she'd be happy I killed you?"

He moaned out loud and his cock twitched in my hand before stream after stream of hot semen spurted from the tip. He hadn't listened to a word that I said. A pity for him. I reached up with my left hand and pulled a knife from under the pillow. He hadn't noticed. Too busy enjoying the final twitches of his tired cock. I waited a second, or two, for him to come out of his moment. When he did, he slowly opened his eyes and looked to me. A smile on his face. A smile on his face that faded when he saw the knife.

"What the fuck?"

"This is for your wife…"

He sat up and promptly fell back against the bed when I plunged the knife into his chest. I didn't pull it out. Just left it there for him. He was gasping. His face was contorted from the pain. I - on the other hand - was smiling the first real smile I'd shown in our time together. I pulled the blade from his chest and watched in awe as blood so easily pumped from the wound. He doesn't have long.

"Your wife's next partner will love her more than you could ever have believed possible. In time - she won't remember your face, she won't remember your name, she won't remember the sound of your voice. No one will remember you..."

⊼

Jon's eyes were closed still. With my spare hand I unbuttoned his trousers. He moaned for me to stop again. This time I listened but only long enough to pull both trousers and underwear down, freeing his penis. He went to move so I shoved him back again before I dropped to my knees and slipped him into my mouth. He sighed out loud again.

"Do you like this? You can cum in my mouth if you want. Let me taste you..." I purred between sucks. "Or you can have my arse. Don't usually offer it but... I'll let you, if that's what you want. If that's what you need..."

I felt his hands either side of my head. He pushed me away a moment but didn't let go of my head. I looked up at him. He was looking down at me. A confused, almost scared, look mixed with the lust he was feeling for me written all over his face.

"I want your cum," I told him.

He pulled me back towards his cock and I greedily slid it down my throat.

When I first started this job - I did what was asked for me with no sexual gratification for myself. It was a way of paying the bills and keeping a roof over my head. I didn't want to go back on the streets again. I'd been there before and it was terrifying. If I had to sell my body to keep from the cold - so be it. As the months went on though, and my job role turned from 'whore' to the role I find myself today - I found I did get some sexual gratification. The thought of killing these men, the cheats, the assholes, the ones who destroy families... The thought of disposing of them turned me on. Funny. Despite ending up killing them - the ones who did have the partners at home, the ones who were to die... They got a better ride than the innocent ones I let survive the appointment, the ones - you could argue - who actually deserved a good fuck.

Jon pulled back and his cock slipped from my mouth. Once again I expected him to pull his trousers back up and run from the room shouting that he was sorry but he said nothing. I looked up to his face. There was no confusion there. No awkwardness. Just lust. He pushed me back and I lost my balance, ending up on the kitchen floor. He stroked himself as he lowered his body over mine - his spare hand ripping at the dressing gown cord loosely tied around my waist. He threw the gown open revealing the underwear I was wearing underneath. No words were needed. I pulled my knickers to one side, exposing my bare cunt to him.

"Do it!" I ordered him.

He didn't need telling twice. He lowered himself over me and pushed inside. I gasped at the feeling. Not as ready as I would have liked to have been. His whole weight pushed down upon me as he slowly started to fuck me. Face to face, he kissed me. His tongue probing my mouth, my tongue meeting his. His hand on my covered breast. I helped him out by pulling my bra down exposing my hardened nipples. When he noticed what I had done, he bent down and suckled on each nipple in turn as he continued to pound me. He stopped suckling and straightened up again so that our heads were side by side. His mouth near to my ear, mine near to his as I sighed breathily. He started to increase the rhythm with which he fucked me. I couldn't help but to run my hands down his back, digging my nails in as they neared the bottom. He yelped out but didn't stop what he was doing - so carried away in the moment that he didn't care he was barebacking. I couldn't help but wonder whether he'd at least wash my cunt juices off his cock before potentially offering it up to his partner. And then I started thinking of putting a knife through him again and again - thoughts which replayed themselves over and over as an intense orgasm started to build within me.

The client lit up a cigarette without asking whether I minded or indeed wanted one. Not a smoker, ideally I would have preferred him to wait until I had left his house before sparking up but I didn't say anything. I couldn't. An outcall appointment to his house; it was up to him what he did. Up to him whether he gave himself lung cancer.

He threw the condom off onto the floor and wiped his dick on the duvet before giving me a wink as though he were proud of his actions or thought he were something special.

"Did you cum?" he asked.

I was sitting on the edge of the bed, pulling my black satin knickers up. I turned around to face him. My eyes were immediately drawn to the bedside cabinet. In particular - the picture of him standing with his wife on what must have been their wedding day given the fact she was in her white dress and the background of the shot was a church.

"You were amazing," I inflated his ego.

Of course I hadn't had an orgasm. I never did on normal appointments. Especially when - every time I turned my head to the side - I saw a picture of the woman I was forced to betray due to the fact I wasn't able to free her from her cheating spouse.

"In fact - if you ever fancy an incall appointment - I'll give you fifty percent off... But it has to be our secret."

I winked at him.

⚓

I screamed as a powerful orgasm washed over me. I felt my face flush as my body shuddered. By the time it had finished, I opened my eyes and realised Jon had pulled away from me slightly - his eyes fixed upon me, watching me experience my private moment of pleasure. He smiled at me.

I took the opportunity to slide him out of me. Before he knew what was happening I was wriggling from underneath him until I was able to turn him over with me on top of him; his back on the cold kitchen floor. I took a hold of his cock and slid it inside of me. Not as much of a sting this time and we both sighed.

"Does your girlfriend fuck you like this?"

I put my hands down on his chest, for added balance, and started rocking backwards and forwards, up and down - the occasional rotation of my hips as I ground down upon him to really milk his cock. He couldn't take his eyes off my body as I fucked him. There was no trace of memory of his girlfriend on his face at all. In this moment - at this time - she simply didn't exist. And that was why he needed to die. She needed someone who cared for her. She needed someone who wouldn't hurt her. He groaned loudly as I increased rhythm.

"You like me fucking you like this? You like the feel of my cunt gripping your cock?"

He didn't answer me. His hands worked their way under my dressing gown and rested upon my buttocks, giving them a squeeze.

"Don't stop. Fuck me!" he demanded.

The monster's hands grabbed the young lady's buttocks and squeezed them hard as she continued to ride him. He demanded that she fucked him. Warned her not to stop despite the tears running down her cheeks as she rode him.

I covered Jon's mouth with my hand to keep him from talking, keep him from reminding me of my past. Don't need to hear those distant memories now. With my other hand, I reached up and steadied myself against the side of the kitchen. Hand pressed against the side, fingers stretched onto the worktop. Small finger resting against the blade of one of my many knives. I little stretch and I could lay my entire hand upon the blade.

Whore's hand reaches under the pillow the client's head rests upon. Knife waiting.

Whore's hand stretches down to under the bed, as client is distracted with tastes of her vaginal fluids. Knife waiting.

Knife under the bed. Knife under the pillow. Always a knife close to hand.

Jon's body twitched underneath me and his legs bucked. He sat up and wrapped his arms around my body, pulling my hand away from the knife in the process. He held me close as the final spasm of the orgasm rocked through his body. This was the part of the appointment when the client tells me how amazing I am, how I'm the best fuck they've ever had, how I was worth every penny, how they wished they had met me in the real world and not within the industry. They'd then take a moment - or two - to remind themselves that there was a strong possibility I wouldn't even look at them out there in what they called the real world. They were right, not that I'd ever tell them.

I rested my head on Jon's shoulder as I looked towards the knife resting on the kitchen work-top, begging to be grabbed. Just as soon as he lets go, it's mine.

"I'm sorry," he said.

I realised he was crying. I thought his body was twitching because of the powerful orgasm he'd experienced but I was wrong. His shoulders were moving because he was crying. Well this is new.

"I'm sorry," he repeated himself as he buried his head against my chest.

Ah. The post-coital guilt. Not quite as common as the men who are busy wishing they could be with me and stating how great I was in bed as soon as they ejaculate; these are the men who feel nothing but guilt for what they have done. Whether it's the fact they'd cheated on their partner or the fact they'd spent money they couldn't really afford on me. Sometimes, even, it was guilt for simply going with a lady such as me. The most insulting line being that they'll need to book themselves in for a test, as though I am carrying some terrible STD - and that's despite the fact that I make them wear a condom. Jon wasn't the first and he won't be the last to feel guilty about what he'd done. I just wondered where his guilt was coming from.

Can't reach the knife, might as well continue the pretense that I give a shit; I held him tight.

"What's wrong?" I asked him.

"I shouldn't have done that," he said. "You shouldn't have done that..."

His words stirred up unwanted memories.

B E F O R E

The monster sat on the edge of the bed with a towel wrapped around his waist. A smile on his face as the young lady stood before him, dressed in a tight black skirt which only just covered her buttocks. A black top - covering her small breasts - which stopped just above her belly button. She turned for him so the monster could see from all angles. Perfectly flat stomach, good figure, tight arse, hair tied into a pony-tail. No make-up. Make-up isn't for young girls. The monster said so.

"Do you like your new clothes?" his voice was quiet. A low growl.

The young girl faced forward and nodded. Even if she hadn't liked them, she wouldn't have said. She preferred the monster's low growl to his deep roar - or even his sharp bite.

"Turn around," he ordered her.

The young girl turned on the spot. Her back to the monster. Facing the wall, she couldn't see him lick his lips.

"So fucking sexy," he growled.

She didn't say anything.

"Touch the floor."

Young body so flexible. The young girl touched the floor with no problems.

"Stay there."

She stayed, arse pointing towards the monster. The skirt rode up, revealing her white knickers previously hidden beneath. She kept her eyes closed as the monster dropped the towel to the floor and started to stroke himself. She heard what he was doing; the sound of his hand rubbing his own dick, the sound of his now-heavy breathing. A few more tugs and he stood up and walked across the small room of their shared apartment before dropping to his knees just behind the young lady. He put his face against her arse and breathed in her scent as he continued to rub himself.

"So fucking sexy, he repeated himself. The low growl considerably more breathy.

The young lady moved away from the monster, just a touch, and the low growl turned to a roar.

"Don't fucking move!"

He pulled her back towards him and held her arse close against his face, pressing his nose between her buttocks. He breathed in deeply again, refusing to let go. Another deep breath and the monster moved one hand from her waist back down to his penis. The stroking resumed, as did the heavy breathing.

"Don't fucking move again," he warned her.

The monster's other hand moved from the young girl's waist down to his scrotum. A few gentle, teasing squeezes as he continued wanking. The young girl took the opportunity to stand up and run towards the front door, just a little way down the hallway. The monster was quick to his feet and right behind her.

"Where the fuck do you think you're going?" he roared.

His voice echoed throughout the small apartment.

The young lady reached the front door and pulled it open only for the monster to reach over her and slam it shut again. He grabbed her by the hair and spun her around before slamming her back against the very same door she had tried to leave from.

"You shouldn't have done that!" he roared. A piece of spit flew from his mouth, hitting her on the cheek. "You shouldn't have done that!"

"I'm sorry!" she screamed.

"Where would you go? What would you do?"

The young girl wept, "I want to go home!"

"This is your home now! Your mother's dead because of what you did with me. You killed your mother. This is your home now," he said again.

He released the young lady's hair and she dropped to the floor into a small ball. Her weeping getting louder. The monster took a hold of her head and pulled her close, forcing his penis into her mouth.

"Earn your keep…"

The young lady didn't have a choice but to swallow the load - a moment that was nearly ruined by a knocking at the door.

PART FIVE

15 YEARS LATER

<u>Guilt</u>

Jon was slamming his fist into the wooden floor out of - I guess - frustration. The banging echoing throughout the room.

"We shouldn't have done that!"

I didn't correct him as there was no need but I had had every right to have done what we did. It was my job. He was the one who shouldn't have done it. He was the one in the wrong. Not me.

"I'm really sorry," he continued.

"You're sorry?"

Was his apology aimed at me or was he just making a general statement? I tried to look him in the face but he pulled me close as though he didn't want the eye contact. Bigger problem with that, though, was that I couldn't reach the knife on the side all the time he kept me close to him.

I've been nice to him this long. A little longer won't kill me, I guess.

"We shouldn't have done that," he said again.

"Because of your girlfriend?" I asked him.

He hesitated a moment before agreeing.

"Yes."

"You're feeling guilty?"

"Yes."

"Well - as you said - that's good. It means you do love her."

He didn't say anything.

"That was your logic," I continued, "if you went with someone such as me and you felt guilty afterwards - it meant you loved your partner. If you didn't feel anything, it meant you didn't love her…"

I still wasn't convinced with his line of thinking. All I knew was that he was a cheat.

"You feel guilty?"

"I feel sick."

"Well - thanks…"

"No. Sorry. I didn't mean that. I just…" he started to cry. "Shouldn't have done it…"

He loosened his other arm from me and I managed to pull away. As soon as he realised I had pulled away, he turned his head to continue avoiding my eye-contact.

I kept my voice low and soothing, "I see a lot of people like you," I told him.

I want to reassure him. I want him to believe everything is going to be okay. I want to make it as such because I want to see the change in his face - the relief through to the panic when I plunge the knife into him. For me to feel fulfilled I need to see that moment. I need it just as he needs to die and his partner needs to be freed from him.

"I doubt it," he said.

His voice - whimpering. Pathetic.

"Look at me," I told him. A sterner voice when he ignored my first instruction, "I said look at me."

He looked at me.

"I've seen many men who feel the way you do after an appointment. The guilt hits them hard - for whatever reason. You're not the only one and you won't be the last either."

I sat up slightly and he slipped out of me, along with a pool of his semen. He cringed as it was another reminder of the sin he thought he had committed.

"I wish you didn't feel like this," I told him.

A strange feeling. There's something bugging me. It's not that I wish he didn't just feel this guilt now but rather - I wish he hadn't had a partner. I wish

I didn't have to kill him. Up until that point - he seemed like a nice person. Quiet, yes. But nice. Pleasant. Friendly. Attentive. It's strange - and hard to explain - but I felt closer to him than I had felt to anyone for a long, long time and I'm not sure why. No sense dwelling on it. He's a cheat. Leopards don't change their spots.

"I shouldn't have come here..."

He tried to push me off. No doubt so he could get up and run back to his partner at home. A quick wash in their bathroom before pretending to be the perfect boyfriend. She'd ask if he had had a good day. He'd say he had. They might even share a kiss. Nothing heavy - just a peck. I wonder - when that happens - can the other half taste me on their boyfriends? Can they smell any trace of perfume which may linger on their skin? Do they sleep with their girlfriends when they get home too? Fuck them just after they've had me? Show off some of the new skills I could have taught them? The thought of them playing happy families, especially knowing I'm not the only woman they've probably gone with... It makes me fucking sick.

"No. You shouldn't have."

The anger was taking hold of me. It was evident in my tone.

"What?"

He looked at me - shocked by the change in tone.

"Your excuse to come and see me? Testing yourself to see if you truly love your partner? It's pathetic. If I'm going to be honest - probably the worst I have heard yet."

"I... I don't understand."

"You came to see me because you wanted to get your end away. Nothing more, nothing less. You wanted a fuck. Woke up horny, thought you'd sample something new. Chickened out yesterday because you knew it was wrong to cheat on your partner but today - showed your true colour..."

"No, that's not it..."

"No? Then what is it? Enlighten me..."

"I just shouldn't have come here. I'm sorry."

I stood up, leaving him on the floor. I leaned back against the kitchen work-top. My hand close to the knife, ready to grab it when I needed to.

"So what do you plan to do with the rest of your day then?"

He sat up, "I don't know…"

"Maybe go home to your girlfriend? Maybe go and hold her? Perhaps you could tell her how much you love her?"

He hesitated. His mind clearly troubled.

"I guess," he said.

"You guess."

"And then - in a few weeks - you'll start to crave my pussy again…"

"What? No."

"You'll wish I was touching you."

"No."

"You'll wish I was riding you. Fucking you."

"Please…"

"You'll be wishing I was kissing you…"

"No. I won't…"

"Because you're all the same."

I grabbed him by his spent penis, and squeezed. He grimaced in pain.

"You're hurting me…"

"You all just think with this."

"That's not what I was doing…"

"But I can help…"

He grabbed my wrist and tried to ease my hand from his dick. I didn't fight him. He was so busy struggling with my hand he didn't notice my other hand grab for the knife. In the blink of an eye I swiped down to his member. He screamed in pain as the blade slice through skin. With wide eyes, he looked down. I already knew I had cut him. I could feel the blood spurting onto my hand. Warm. I looked down too. The knife wasn't sharp enough to cut right the way through but it had sliced it wide open. I let go and he dropped to the floor holding his junk - as though trying to stop it from falling off completely, or stopping the blood from pumping out. He was breathing heavy. Hard. Panic set in. That won't help him.

"Without those, you might all start behaving properly. Like gentlemen should."

He was gasping like a fish out of water. Between gasps, begging me to call for help… I didn't tell him I wouldn't be making the call. I don't think I needed to.

"Hurts doesn't it? Well, don't worry, I'm pretty sure it won't hurt for long. That's a lot of blood you're losing… But remember this - you brought this all onto yourself… You cheated on your girlfriend. You cheated, this is the cost. As I've said before - you're not the first and you won't be the last."

He was shaking his head as he gasped.

"No girlfriend… no girlfriend…" he kept saying the same thing again and again.

"What? What do you mean?"

Did he mean he didn't have a girlfriend?

"No girlfriend…" - still gasping. Weak voice. Pale face.

"What are you talking about?"

I wanted to scream at him so that he'd explain himself but I knew it would do no good. His eyes were shut now as he continued to writhe around on the kitchen floor due to the substantial pain he was in. I looked down and noticed his blood was inching closer and closer to my bare feet. I stepped back, still with the knife in hand.

"No girlfriend…"

"Stop saying that!" I screamed.

I lunged forward at him with the knife and plunged it into his throat until my hand (still on the handle) was touching his skin. His eyes were so wide I thought they were going to pop directly from his skull. I pulled the blade out, with a little struggle, and was hit in the face by a jet of blood. I stepped back again, wiping my face. He closed his eyes and his head tilted to one side. The blood now nothing more than a trickle. I'm not sure why he kept repeating himself again and again and I didn't want to know. He must have had a girlfriend at home. He wouldn't have been the first person to try and tell me there wasn't one - just to try and save himself…

𝝠

"Please. I didn't mean it. I don't have a girlfriend at home. I don't. I just… I said it because I didn't want you thinking I was a loser… Please…"

The client looked weak as he struggled against the restraints as I gently pressed the tip of the knife's blade against his chest, ready to pierce the chest and heart.

"Please... You're my first... I promise... I'll go... Never come back... Not to you or any other girl... Please..."

It's funny listening to the excuses come out when they know what's coming. Reminds me that - when all is said and done - men really are the weaker of the species.

⚔

My first impression of Jon had been that he could well have been a virgin but I can't think of him as such. I need to think of him as having a girlfriend at home; a partner who he cheated on. If I start thinking of him as being single - having lied to me... Doesn't even bear thinking about it. He was a cheat. That's it. He was an asshole and I saved his girlfriend.

I dropped the knife to the floor and surveyed the mess before me. He's gone now. Out of his misery. He was lucky. He got off light. Deserved more for what he was putting his girlfriend through. If she existed. Stop thinking like that. She existed. She's real. He wasn't lying to me - not at the start anyway. He just wanted to try and save himself. Fuck him. He got what he deserved.

So much blood all over the floor. Shouldn't have done this here. Should have done it upstairs on the bed. Easier to clean than down here and certainly easier to get him to the bathroom for the cutting.

I looked towards the hallway. No sense dragging him down there and try-ing to get him up the stairs. Probably won't be able to get him up there even if I wanted to. And if I could - it'd just spread the gore further through the house. So much blood in here, so much mess... I may as well keep it contained to the one room. Can have a good bleach throughout when I am done.

I reached down to his ankles and lifted his feet from the bloodied floor. With hands on his trousers, I pulled them from his body spilling the contents of his pockets onto the tiles. Worry about those bits later. Get him dealt with first. As soon as the trousers slipped off his body, his legs thudded back onto the floor, splashing more of the pooling blood up the kitchen sides. Ignore it. Worry about that later too.

I straddled his cooling corpse and pulled him up by his neck. After a bit of a struggle I managed to get his shirt off so that he was naked. Again, I let go and he fell back against the floor hard. Another splash. God damn it. Should have been prepared for this. Should have seen it coming... Should always be prepared.

⋏

I climbed off both the bed and client, onto the floor. I reached under the bed and pulled on a plastic roll of sheeting, stretching it out over the length of the bedroom floor until not a piece of carpet remained uncovered. I headed back over to the bed and walked around the other side before rolling the client onto the floor (and plastic sheeting).

A bit of blood spilled from body to floor but I wasn't worried; plastic sheeting caught it.

⋏

More blood up the sides of the cupboard as I started hacking away at limbs, having fetched the bag of tools from under the bed where I stored them. I tried not to think about it. There was already so much mess, what's a little more?

This was the part of the process I hated. Not because I am squeamish. I had been when I had done it the first time but now I was used to it; the smell, the sight - everything about it. I wished there was another way of dealing with the ex-clients but there wasn't. At least, not one that I could see. Besides - this was by far the safest way I could think of to keep them from being found; cut them up into little pieces and put them in small holes in the garden. Hopefully I'll be long gone before anyone else comes to rent this place and then I could always try and blame a previous occupant if the body parts were discovered. Deny all knowledge. Act dumb and flash a bit of cleavage? Hope that the investigators are male?

⋏

I pulled my car to the side of the road. The blue flashing lights from the silent siren behind me illuminated the night air. I checked in the rear-view mirror and saw the officer climbing from his car. A stupid speed trap. I turned to watch him from the side mirror on the car. Quickly, I leaned forward and undid the seat-belt. A second later - and just in the nick of time - I undid the two buttons of my blouse showing more cleavage than I usually dared (when away from paying clients at least).

The officer knocked on the car window with his torch and motioned for me to wind it down - which I did.

"Good evening," he said as he crouched down to eye level.

I was good enough to look into his eyes and show him a level of respect I thought an officer deserved. He stared down at my cleavage.

"Is there a problem, officer?"

His face reddened when he realised what he was doing. His gaze turned from breast to eye.

"Do you know how fast you were going?" he asked.

"I'm sorry. No."

"38mph... Do you know what the speed limit is here?"

"Yes. I'm sorry."

I fidgeted in my seat, successfully pushing up my cleavage in a move which would have otherwise been viewed as innocent. His eyes slipped down again.

"Can I see your driving licence?" he asked.

I reached into my purse and pulled out my plastic identification. I handed it over to him and he looked at it with the help of his torch. A glance at my face to confirm I was the same person. He smiled at me and handed the I.D back.

"Well - just slow it down," he said.

He licked his lips.

"I will. I'm sorry."

"Don't want you having an accident."

He smiled at me.

"Okay. Thank you."

"Have a good evening," he said.

Another quick look down at my ample cleavage.

"You too."

I wound the window back up as he walked back towards his waiting automobile.

⋏

I wondered whether the cleavage trick would work if they did dig the garden up. I'd better not count on it. I put his arm to one side and placed the blade against his neck. The first few cuts are easy. Similar to how a knife slices through a thin piece of ham as it rips the skin. The next cuts - the deeper ones - are harder as you come across the muscles. Not pleasant either. Probably the worst part for me, in fact.

I pushed down on the blade. Just get on with it. As I pulled back with the saw, his head twisted towards me. His eyes fixed to mine. I stopped what I was doing. Transfixed for a moment by something I couldn't explain. Something about the look in his eye. I pushed his head to face the other direction. Should never look into their eyes when they're dead. Learned that lesson the first time I killed someone. At least I thought I had. It's not what you see in their eyes which turns my stomach and haunts me. It's what you don't see. It's hard to explain but the eyes are the windows to the souls. When there is no soul - there is nothing but darkness there. A darkness caused by me and - more to the point - a darkness that I will one day slip into.

Before Jon revealed he had a girlfriend - there was a kindness in his soul - but that was gone now as made evident by the accidental look into his dead eyes. I did that. Whether it was deserved or not, I did it. I took that soul.

I tried to put it from my mind as I resumed the messy task at hand. Thankfully it didn't take long for the saw to cut its way through - separating head from neck. A few more cuts and we'll be done. He'll be done. Then it's just a question of digging the hole and cleaning up.

I sat back a moment and wiped my brow. So tired. Wish I had been more prepared for this. If only I had had the damned plastic sheet...

⋏

I hurried over to the edge of the plastic sheeting and took hold of it before folding it over the client's body. I walked back to the bed and stripped it off, throwing the dirty sheets on top of the client. Once the bed was stripped I headed to the other side of the plastic sheeting and also folded that over the client - cocooning him in a perfect plastic wrap. Perfect. I walked to the edge closest to the bedroom door and grabbed a handful of plastic laminate. The good thing about having laminate flooring across the upstairs of the house? It made it easy to drag someone wrapped in plastic across it. Well - certainly easier than it could have been and definitely minimal mess. Just a few spots here and there to clean.

My kitchen looked like an abattoir by the time I had bagged up the body pieces in black bin bags kept under the sink. I wanted to get him in the ground to start the - usually fairly easy - process of forgetting about him and moving on with my life; usually into the direction of the next cheating scum. I knew it wasn't that easy though. If I left the mess in here, until last, then it would have just been harder for me to clean up. Wet blood smears and makes a mess of things causing you all kinds of hassle but dry sticky blood really clings onto things and is an absolute nightmare. To stand any chance of getting rid of it you have to soak it again. Once soaked, you start rubbing it and - yep - same process as if you had started with the cleaning when the blood was already dripping.

I filled the washing up bowl with hot soapy water and moved it from sink to floor, next to where the worst of the blood had pooled. A wire scrubbing pad was floating on top of the water along with a sponge. Thankfully I had more of both under the sink as it would take more than just one of each to clean the mess up. I hesitated a moment and looked around. Such a state.

Come on, can't just stand here staring at it - need to clean it. Need to get rid of the gore, dig the holes and bury him once and for all. Be done with it and move on as quickly as my mind lets me - and going by the way his face keeps lingering at the forefront of it; this could take a while.

I sighed heavily and spoke out loud in an effort to motivate myself, "Come on. Need to get this done. Sooner it's done, sooner you can put it to bed…"

"Clean yourself up."

The monster spoke to the young lady as though she were a piece of shit sticking to the sole of his shoe. It was always the same when he had finished what he needed to do. He adjusted his clothes as he tucked his cock back into his pants. The young girl just sat there with her back to the door she had earlier tried to escape from, a spool of semen running down her chin from where she'd not swallowed it all. She didn't speak to him. She didn't argue. She never did. Temptation was great but she knew she couldn't - not with the collection of spunk hiding under her tongue ready for her to spit out at the first given opportunity.

The monster didn't like her spitting. He wanted every drop gulped down as though it were her favourite custard dessert. Extra thick and creamy; reminding her of a 'joke' he once oozed into her ear post-fuck.

"How do you know if a man has a high sperm count? The woman has to chew before she swallows."

She shuddered at the thought. The monster turned his back on her and she got up from the floor, wiping her chin with the back of her still-shaking hand. She headed for the bathroom but stopped dead at the sound of someone banging on their front door. The monster also froze. Another bang and he slowly turned to the door. A quick glance to the girl.

"Get in the bedroom."

Someone - voice unrecognised - called into the apartment from beyond the door. The police. Anger in their tone. Hostility. Another bang on the door shaking it on its hinges.

"Get in the fucking bedroom!" he hissed.

The young lady ran into the bedroom and closed the door. The man composed himself and walked to the front door. He opened it as though there were nothing for him to hide or be ashamed of. Several police officers burst into the apartment - their way paved by a stern looking officer in a suit holding up a badge.

"Mr. Ellis - I'm arresting you for the rape of a minor..."

The officer in charge turned to his uniformed colleagues and told them to find the girl whilst he read the monster his rights. The officers filed down the hallway, sticking their heads into the rooms but they found nothing other than an emptied wallet by an open window. Curtains blowing in the breeze.

⋏

I dragged the bags into the corner of the room by the back door. I didn't want to leave them out back until I was ready to deal with them. People didn't come by this house uninvited but - even so - I couldn't afford to leave the rubbish there just in case…

I unrolled another black big bag and picked up his shirt, dropping it into the ready liner. His underpants were next. I set the bin to one side - on the kitchen work-top - and picked up his trousers. His wallet and keys in the pocket. There was a drain out back which dropped into the sewer; the perfect home for the keys. Not the first set to be lost down there and certainly not the last. The wallet would burn with the clothes later but only after I'd taken the money. Money only, never cards. Cards and all identification, like the wallet, burns easily enough.

I opened the wallet and smiled at the sight of the cash; a nice thick wad. I took the notes out and put it on top of the fridge; the only surface that didn't appear to have a splattering of blood. I pulled out the credit cards and dropped them into the bag with his clothes and… I froze.

My heart was beating hard enough to burst through my ribcage.

"No…"

His face was staring at me from his full driving licence. A slight smile. The kindness in his eyes I'd seen yesterday. Hair combed back like he was trying to make a good impression when he went for the picture to be taken. Next to that his details; date of birth, birth town, first name… His surname…

My surname…

"No…"

Before

The mother slammed the front door to the family home and screamed out loud; loud enough to drown out her daughter's sobbing and begging from behind the door - out in the cold. She looked up and saw him standing there, at the top of the stairs, clutching onto his favourite teddy bear. The front of his pyjamas soaked in urine where he'd wet the bed; too afraid to climb out and go to the toilet due to all the shouting and screaming. Tears rolling down his six year old face as he sobbed.

The mother, still wailing, crawled her way from the front door to the bottom of the stairs. She made it no further before collapsing onto her front in floods of tears. The little boy sat on the stairs and didn't dare move.

⚓

"Don't worry about him, he'll be fine."

The mother's older brother was standing in the very same hallway a day later. By his side was a suitcase filled with some of the boy's clothes and a handful of his favourite toys. The mother had called for help. She couldn't cope with the boy on top of trying to sort her head out. The boy didn't understand just as he didn't understand the noises that used to come from his sister and the monster. He'd just lie there, in his bed, with his eyes scrunched tight for fear of being next on the visitor's list. Now he was standing by his uncle. He recognised the face from family Christmas parties but didn't really know the man. He didn't want to go. He wanted to stay with his mother. She didn't want him. Why didn't she want him?

⋏

Scared little boy lying in an unfamiliar bed. Yet more tears spilling from his eyes and he's told by the uncle he is getting to know that he mother has gone to Heaven. He's promised that everything is going to be okay and he's promised that he is safe now. His aunty standing in the corner of the room - a sympathetic look upon her pale face. Her eyes also red from tears unwanted.

"And we've found your sister," the uncle said, "we're getting her back."

Scared little boy forced a smile. He didn't understand why his mother was shouting at his sister or why his father left the home but he missed them both. If one could come home - it might make things a little easier for him. The uncle ruffled his hair and said he'd be downstairs if he needed anything and that he shouldn't be afraid to come and see him. The uncle stood and promised again that everything was going to be okay.

⋏

The little boy awoke to see his uncle standing by the side of his bed. A sad expression on his face and news on his lips that his sister wouldn't be coming home right away but - hopefully - soon instead. The little boy didn't say anything. He just nodded. He didn't know why she wasn't coming home right away and wondered if it was because she didn't want to see him. He swallowed the thought down and hoped she'd change her mind.

The little boy wasn't the only person who wanted her to come home.

⋏

First night on the street alone and the money stolen from the monster's wallet wasn't enough for a room for the night. A kind stranger had pulled up next to where the young lady was standing and asked if she were okay. He offered her a seat in his car to warm herself up and asked her what was wrong when he saw the look on her face. The young lady explained she'd run away and that she couldn't go home. She explained - spilling her guts - that she didn't have enough money to stay anywhere and the man smiled at her. He said that everything was going to be okay and showed her a wallet full of cash. He asked if she wanted to earn some for herself and the young lady - already aware she was in the presence of another monster - asked what needed to be done.

The man replied with a smile.

EPILOGUE

15 Years Later

His name was James

dropped to my knees and screamed as I read the driving licence again. It couldn't be right. It couldn't be. I pulled the black bag from the kitchen work-top down to the floor with me and fished out the credit cards. It's not right. It's a sick joke. That's it. A sick joke someone is playing on me. The cards will prove that. I looked at the first one and then the second - both had the same name. James Ellis. I screamed again that they were wrong. It couldn't be him. It couldn't. There's no reason as to why he would be here with me. There's no reason why he would have let me…

I gagged as I recalled our time spent together. I threw up when I felt a little bit of him trickle from between my legs. It's not possible. It's not him. He was only six when I left. He was only six. This couldn't be him. I threw up again as I recalled the taste of his cock in my mouth. Another scream as I remembered the look on his face when I swiped down with the blade…

Please God no!

Everything was piecing together in my head. Bit by painful bit…

The times he'd pull away at my touch.

The questions he asked - not just about what I do but about my family.

The fact he got embarrassed and ran from the appointment when I made a move.

No.

Why hadn't I recognised him?

I refuse to believe it.

It's not him.

It's a sick joke.

It has to be.

I picked the identification back up and looked at the picture. Even now I know it was him - I don't recognise him. How the years have changed him. It can't be him. Please don't let it be him. Please… My mind taunting me with how he felt inside of me, the fact that I felt a connection to him I hadn't felt for many years… The look on his face when I slashed him with the knife. His final words. No. Please.

"No girlfriend! No girlfriend!"

The whole reason he had come to me was a lie. His final words letting me know he wasn't a cheat. Was he ever going to tell me his true intentions for coming? Why didn't he say something before anything happened? It could have all been avoided! What was he so scared of? So many questions to remain unanswered. His final words trying to tell me why he'd come here. Why couldn't he just say something? Oh God. The regret he felt after he came. Why didn't he stop me? Why'd he go through with it?

I threw up on the floor.

Kitchen of blood and puke.

Why did he let me do it? Why did he let me believe he was one of them? I threw up again.

Why did he come and find me?

How did he find me?

I screamed as loud as I could. A scream which echoed through the quiet empty home.

THE END

A Plea From The Author:

Well hello you! The fact you're reading this suggests you made it to the end of my book. I hope that you enjoyed reading it as much as I enjoyed writing it. Whether you did - or whether you didn't - I would like to take the time to say a massive thank you for giving my work a go. It really does mean the world to me and there aren't enough words in the world for me to express as much. Without you - the readers - I am nothing more than a mad monkey sitting at a keyboard frantically bashing away at the sticking keys.

If you would like to find out more about me - as an author and a person - feel free to get in touch on Facebook (www.facebook.com/mattshawpublications). I love the interaction with you guys. I'm sure you can understand it gets incredibly lonely sitting at a computer day in and day out working on these so it's nice to break it up with a little bit of social interaction and general madness!

Now - if you enjoyed this story - and would like to help me out a little, then you could think about leaving a review on Amazon, Goodreads, or anywhere else that readers visit. The most important part of how well a book sells is how many positive reviews it has, so if you leave me one then you are directly helping me to continue on this mad journey. And - for those who do manage to leave a review for me - a great, big massive thanks in advance and, as a little bonus, feel free to copy it to my Facebook Page for a chance to be brutally murdered in my next story...

Anyway, that's me done! Once again thank you for your time and I really hope you enjoyed what you read.

Kind Regards,
Matt Shaw

OTHER TITLES FROM MATT SHAW

<u>Extreme</u>

Sick Bastards
SickER Bastards
Psychopath For Hire
PORN
WHORE
TORTURED
Rotting Dead F*cks
ART (co-written with Michael Bray)

<u>Serial Killer Books</u>

CLOWN
Consumed

The Peter Chronicles broken down in order
Happy Ever After (book one)
G.S.O.H Essential (book two)
A Fresh Start (book three)
PETER (book four)

All Good Things (book five)
Once Upon a Time (book six)

9 Months Book 1
9 Months Book 2
9 Months Book 3

<u>Supernatural books</u>

The Cabin
The Cabin II: Asylum
The Cabin Books (books 1 and 2 collection)
A House in the Country
The Lost Son
Heaven Calling
The Missing Years of Thomas Prichard
Bitten

<u>Psychological Horror</u>
Control
Love Life
SEED
Evil Lurking Within
Smile
The Infestation
Buried
The 8th
Romance is Dead
The Chosen Routes
The Last Stop
Writer's Block

Short Stories
My Deadly Obsession
The Breakdown
Influenza: Strain 'Z'

Collections

9 Months Trilogy
Happy Ever After Volume One (Peter Chronicles books 1-3)
Happy Ever After Volume Two (Peter Chronicles books 4-6)
Tastes of Horror (Smile, The 8th, The Cabin, Happy Ever After, Buried, The Ward)
Scribblings From a Dark Place (collection of short stories and access to film MENU)
A Taste of Fears 1 (short stories based on readers' fears)
A Taste of Fears 2 (short stories based on readers' fears)
The Story Collection: Volume One (The Last Stop, The Chosen Routes, Writer's Block, Smile, Love Life)
The Story Collection: Volume Two (Buried, The Dead Don't Knock, The Breakdown, Romance is Dead)

Real Life

PlentyofFreaks
im fine
Still fine
Self Publishing: Releasing your book to the Digital Market
Wasting Stamps

Choose Your Own Adventure

A Christmas to Remember

Children's Stories

The Vampire's Treaty

Picture Books

I Hate Fruit & Veg

16437995R00061